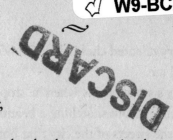

Dear Reader,

I love reading books that are set in places where I've lived. It's more than just knowing the street names—I love recognizing the individual vibrancy and feel of each unique American city.

As a writer, I've likewise loved setting my books in places that are familiar to me, and this book, *Stand-in Groom,* is set in my beloved town of Boston, Massachusetts.

I first visited Boston as a teenager, and fell in love with the history and the weirdly winding downtown roads that used to be cow paths, and okay, yes, the vibrant music scene. (Some trivia: For several years I earned a living playing my guitar and singing in Boston's underground T [subway] stations.)

When Johnny Anziano, the hero of *Stand-in Groom,* first "walked" into my office all those years ago when I sat down to write this book, I recognized right away that he was a creative type but, surprisingly, not a musician. No, Johnny was a very talented chef, which immediately intrigued me.

Johnny's story begins when he stops some teenage thugs from snatching a beautiful woman's purse in the streets of the city that both he and I love.

I'm delighted that Bantam has reissued *Stand-in Groom*. I hope you enjoy this visit to Boston as much as I enjoyed writing it!

Love,

Suzanne Brockmann

Suz

## BY SUZANNE BROCKMANN

### TROUBLESHOOTERS SERIES
The Unsung Hero
The Defiant Hero
Over the Edge
Out of Control
Into the Night
Gone Too Far
Flashpoint
Hot Target
Breaking Point
Into the Storm
Force of Nature
All Through the Night
Into the Fire
Dark of Night
Hot Pursuit

### SUNRISE KEY SERIES
Kiss and Tell
The Kissing Game
Otherwise Engaged

### OTHER BOOKS
Heartthrob
Forbidden
Freedom's Price
Body Language
Stand-In Groom
Time Enough for Love

# SUZANNE BROCKMANN

# *Stand-in Groom*

BANTAM BOOKS
NEW YORK

*Stand-in Groom* is a work of fiction. Names, characters, places, and incidents are the products of the author's imagination or are used fictitiously. Any resemblance to actual events, locales, or persons, living or dead, is entirely coincidental.

2009 Bantam Books Mass Market Edition

Copyright © 1997 by Suzanne Brockmann

Published in the United States by Bantam Books, an imprint of The Random House Publishing Group, a division of Random House, Inc., New York.

Bantam Books is a registered trademark of Random House, Inc., and the colophon is a trademark of Random House, Inc.

Originally published in mass market in the United States by Bantam Books, a division of Random House, Inc., in 1997.

ISBN 978-0-553-59312-9

Cover photograph: Getty Images/Schultheiss Selection GmbH & CoKG
Cover design and photo manipulation: Lynn Andreozzi

Printed in the United States of America

www.bantamdell.com

2 4 6 8 9 7 5 3 1

For Melanie and Jason

# ONE

CHELSEA WAS BEING followed.

It was crazy.

True, this wasn't the best neighborhood in Boston, but it was seven o'clock in the morning. It was broad daylight.

She glanced behind her. There were three of them—lean, dangerous-looking young men dressed in gang colors. She slipped the strap of her purse securely around her neck as she moved more quickly down the sidewalk. She could be wrong. Maybe they were heading toward the H&R Block that was three doors down from her office.

Maybe they were looking to have their taxes done.

They were right behind her now, and she moved aside, toward the street, praying that they would walk on past.

They didn't.

"Hey, blondie." The taller of the three leered at her—if it was possible for a sixteen-year-old to leer.

They were only kids. Kids with fuzz on their upper lips and chins that was supposed to pass as facial hair. Kids pretending to be grown men. Kids who were taller and wider than she was. Kids who probably carried knives and could hurt her badly before she could even shout for help.

"You part of the beautification program in this part of the city?" the shortest of the three asked, laughing at his own joke. He wore an enormous ring in his nose—obviously to make up for his lack of height. He couldn't have been more than fourteen years old.

The third boy made animal noises—part dog, part barnyard pig—as he invaded her personal space.

Chelsea stepped out between two parked cars,

into the street. "Excuse me. I need to get to work, and you should probably get to school—"

She had to stop short to keep from bumping into the tall one.

"Excuse me," he mimicked her. "Excuse me. We don't go to no friggin' school."

"Maybe you should reconsider. You could use a little help with your grammar." She stepped around him, but the dog-boy blocked her path. He grinned, and she pulled back. His teeth were all filed to sharp little points. He snorted and woofed at her obvious alarm.

That's all they wanted. They wanted to scare her. Well, okay. She was scared. They could let her go now.

"You got some money we can borrow?" the nose-ring wearer asked. "We'll pay you back—we promise."

She felt a flash of anger, wondering how often that had worked—how often the people they intimidated simply handed over their money.

As the other boys laughed Chelsea pushed past them onto the sidewalk, aware of the cars moving down the street, aware that not a single one of them had even slowed to see if she needed help.

"Go away," she said sharply, "before I call your mothers."

It was the wrong thing to say.

The dog-boy pushed her, hard, and she went down onto her knees. The tall one grabbed the strap of her purse and it lifted her back up as it caught around her throat.

He was running now, all three of them were, and she was dragged and bounced along the cracked, uneven sidewalk. She heard herself screaming and she felt her shoe come off, felt her toes scrape along the concrete. Her head snapped back and her arm twisted behind her as the boy yanked her bag free.

God! All the work she did at home last night—that flash drive was in her purse! Chelsea pushed herself up off the sidewalk, kicked off her other shoe, and ran after them.

They were nearly a block ahead of her, but she could think of nothing but all those hours of work, and she ran faster.

And then it happened.

With a squeal of tires, a white delivery truck bounced over the curb, right onto the sidewalk in front of the three kids. The driver swung himself out the open door of the cab, landing directly on top of the tallest boy. The kid was no match for a full-grown man, and the truck driver was *extremely* full grown. All it took was an almost nonchalant backhanded blow, and the big kid went down, her shoulderbag pulled free from his hands.

But the dog-boy and the kid with the nose-ring were both behind the man. Chelsea saw a glint of sunlight reflect off the blade of a knife.

"Look out!" she shouted, and the man turned. The way he moved was graceful, like a choreographed dance, as he disarmed the kid with a well-placed sweep of his foot. He moved threateningly toward the dog-boy, who turned tail and ran after his friends.

Chelsea slowed to a stop, aware that her heart was pounding, that her panty hose were torn, her clothes askew, her hair loosened from her usual French braid and dangling around her shoulders, aware that the soles of her feet burned and stung from her shoeless run down the rough city sidewalk. She had to bend over to catch her breath, hands braced above her bruised knees.

She tilted her head to look up at the man who'd rescued her handbag. He looked even taller from this position, his shoulders impossibly broad. He was dressed in well-faded blue jeans and worn white leather athletic shoes. He wore a Boston Red Sox cap backward over a dark head of unruly curls and a T-shirt that proclaimed in large red letters I'M TOO SEXY FOR MY SHIRT. Given a leather jacket and a studded dog collar, he could have been those kids' older and far more dangerous brother.

"You all right?" he asked her, moving closer, his dark eyes even darker with concern. "You need me to call the paramedics?"

Chelsea shook her head no, taking quick stock of her bruises and scrapes. Both knees were bleeding slightly, as were both elbows and the heel of one hand. The top of her right foot and most of those toes were sore. Her neck felt raw where the strap of her purse had given her a burn.

"I'm okay." She straightened up, trying to tuck her blouse back into her skirt, trying to ignore the fact that her hands were shaking so hard, she couldn't get the job done.

The man didn't ignore it. "Maybe you should sit down."

Chelsea nodded. Sit down. That would be good. She let him lead her across the sidewalk to a building that had a stone stairway going up to the front entrance. He helped her sit on the third step up, then sat next to her, setting her handbag between them and pulling off his baseball cap.

She glanced at him, aware that he was gazing at her.

He wasn't what she'd call classically handsome. His nose was big and crooked, as if it had been broken one too many times. His cheekbones were rugged and angular, showcasing a pair of liquid-brown, heavily lidded eyes. His mouth was generously wide, with full, sensuous lips that seemed on the verge of a smile. His hair was dark and curly and long, and as he steadily returned her curious gaze he pulled it back into a ponytail at the nape of his neck.

"I've seen you around the neighborhood for a couple of weeks," he told her. His voice was deep and husky, with more than a hint of urban Boston coloring it. "You opened up that computer consulting business around the corner, right?"

She nodded. She hadn't seen *him* around. She would've remembered. "I'm Chelsea Spencer." She held out her hand.

"I know," he said, finally letting his smile loose as he gently clasped her fingers.

It was a smile that was set on heavy stun. Chelsea was not normally affected by such things, but this man's smile was off the scale. It was a smile that seemed to echo the words on his T-shirt. She glanced at those words again. He followed her gaze and actually blushed, a delicate shade of pink tingeing his rugged cheekbones.

"A friend got me this shirt," he explained sheepishly. "I'm visiting him today, and I wore it, you know, kind of like a joke?" He was still holding her hand. "I'm Giovanni Anziano. My friends call me Johnny."

"Thank you for saving my bag."

His smile faded as his gaze swept her scraped knees and dirt-streaked clothes. "I wish I got there sooner. They didn't do more than knock you over, did they?"

He was watching her closely. His eyes may have been lazily hooded, but Chelsea got the sense that this man missed nothing. She shook her head. "No."

He ran one hand down his face. "Jeez, will you listen to me? 'They didn't do more than knock you over'—as if that wasn't enough. I saw you bounce when you hit the ground. You sure you don't want some professional help getting cleaned up? There's a hospital not too far from here and it won't take too long."

"Oh, no!" Chelsea pulled her hand free and closed her eyes. "Oh, God, I've got a meeting with a client in an hour." She laughed, but it sounded faintly hysterical, so she stopped. "I look like I've been hit by a train."

"You look like you've been mugged."

Chelsea stood, searching the street for a taxi. "If I hurry, I can take a cab home and get cleaned up and only be a few minutes late." She turned to face him. "Thank you again. If you hadn't come to my rescue..."

Johnny stood up, too, and again she was startled by how very tall he was. "Lookit, I'm running a little early. Hop in the truck, and I'll give you a ride home and back."

She gazed at him in surprise. He laughed, as if he could read the trepidation in her eyes.

"I'm not dangerous," he told her. "I promise. Come on, I work for Meals on Wheels, delivering food to helpless little old ladies who unlock their apartment doors for me without batting an eye. Hell, I've got a key ring the size of New Hampshire for all the people who can't get up to answer their own door."

Meals on Wheels. The words were painted on the side of the truck that was still parked in the middle of the sidewalk. Meals on Wheels was a charity organization that delivered precooked meals to shut-ins. Some of them were ill, some elderly, all of them unable either to get to a grocery store or cook their own meals for whatever reason. Whoever this Giovanni Anziano was, the Meals on Wheels organization trusted him enough to allow him to make deliveries.

He smiled again, and Chelsea felt her stomach flip-flop. She could imagine him smiling at her that way as he leaned over to kiss her, as he pulled her against that rock-solid body, encircling her with those powerful arms. She could imagine him smiling at her as he helped her out of her clothes and...

Where on earth had *that* thought come from? She wasn't prone to having on-the-spot fantasies about strange men—no matter what they looked like. No matter if they were, indeed, too sexy for their shirts.

"Hop in," Johnny said again. "I'll go get your shoes."

Chelsea Spencer.

She was sitting in the Meals on Wheels truck. She was sitting next to him, holding tightly to her bag as he took the right turn onto Beacon Street, heading out toward Brookline, where she lived.

Johnny glanced at her again, smiling as he met her eyes. Man, she was the definition of incredible.

It was weird, because she wasn't especially pretty—at least not in the conventional sense. Her nose was a touch too pointy, her chin too sharp. But taken with the rest of her face, she was strikingly attractive. Her eyes were a shade of blue Johnny hadn't even known existed before he first caught sight of her. Her hair was silky and golden blond. And her mouth...Her lips were gracefully shaped and gorgeously full. It was the kind of mouth he fantasized about. And God knows he'd been doing a hell of a lot of fantasizing lately....

"I'd been meaning to stop in your office and

introduce myself for a couple of weeks now," he said, pulling up to a red light and turning to look at her.

She glanced at him again, and he could see an answering flash of attraction in her eyes.

He felt his pulse accelerate and forced himself to slow down. He had a shot here. If he asked her out, there was actually a chance that she would accept. But he had to chill out, take it slow, be cool. Be very, very cool.

The light turned green, and he stepped on the gas.

He couldn't believe it when he'd seen the three punks knocking Chelsea down to the ground. And he *really* couldn't believe it when she started chasing after *them*. The lady had guts. When most people were mugged, they got up and ran in the opposite direction. "Are you going to press charges?" he asked.

She snorted. "Of course."

Johnny nodded. "Of course." He tried to hide his smile. "Silly question."

"Will you do me a favor?"

Oh yeah. Especially if it involved full body contact... He nodded again, aware that she was watching him. He forced himself to sound cool. Nonchalant. "Sure."

She smiled. "Don't you want to know what it is first?"

"Nope."

"Hmmm. In that case, maybe I better think about whether there are any other big favors I need done..."

She was flirting. Chelsea Spencer was flirting with him.

"How about we discuss the terms of this favor over dinner tonight?" he countered. There. Damn! He did it. He asked her out.

But she just laughed. "There're no terms. I just need you to file a statement with the police. You probably got as good a look at those guys as I did."

"All right, but..." He shook his head. "Just don't expect the police to be able to do too much with what we tell them."

Her smile faded. "I know there's only a small chance the police will be able to find those boys, but..." She suddenly sat forward in her seat, pointing. "Take the next left. My building's the second on the right."

He followed her instructions and double-parked in front of her building. This block was all high-priced condominiums. The buildings were perfectly maintained, their grounds well kept. It was Nice, with a capital *N*, and a silent but very present dollar sign in front of that capital *N*.

Chelsea Spencer had money. A lot more money than he'd imagined. Johnny gazed up at the ritzy building. It was possible this lady was out of his league. Not that *he* necessarily thought so, but if *she* thought so, the game was over.

Chelsea opened the truck door and turned to look back at him. "I'll be quick."

"Don't be so quick that you forget to wash out those scrapes with soap."

She smiled. "You sound like my mother."

"No, I sound like *my* mother. She was a doctor."

"No kidding."

"Nope."

She was just sitting there, one hand on the opened door, gazing across the truck into his eyes. Johnny gazed back, hardly daring to breathe.

"I'll, um, go change," she said breathlessly.

"I'll be right here."

It took her thirteen and a half minutes.

For thirteen and a half minutes Johnny sat behind the wheel of the truck and planned. He'd take her out to dinner tonight to his restaurant. He rolled his eyes in self-disgust. *His* restaurant? Try, the restaurant in which he worked. *His* restaurant was the one that was still in fantasy form. *His* restaurant was pre-embryonic—an idea, a gleam in his eye, the beginnings of a small fortune in his savings account. But it was only a matter of time before he had enough money to make that dream come true.

But until then, he had to settle for the distinguished title of Head Chef at Lumière's, among the best of Boston's four-star restaurants.

He wasn't on shift tonight, but he could easily go in during the late afternoon and prepare a dinner for two. Veal. Chelsea Spencer would go for veal, in his special sauce and…

Tomorrow he'd meet her for lunch. He'd bring a picnic basket and they'd walk over to the Common, spread out a blanket and a few of his garlic-dijon chicken-salad sandwiches and…

He had to work both Friday and Saturday night, but Sunday he had the entire day off.

Sunday. Sunday, he'd pull out all the stops.

Sunday, he'd seduce her. He'd show up here at her condo early enough in the morning so that she'd still be in her nightgown. He'd bring warm butter croissants and he'd kiss the crumbs from her lips and...

Chelsea quickly descended the front steps of her building, brushing out her long blond hair. She wore flowing, loose-fitting pants and a long-sleeved blouse. A wide belt accentuated her slim waist. No one would've believed she'd been mugged not quite an hour ago.

She smiled as she climbed in the truck. "Police didn't hassle you for double parking?"

He smiled back at her as he started the engine. "Meals on Wheels trucks don't get hassled."

She fastened her seat belt and began braiding her hair. "I don't know how I can thank you for doing this."

It was the perfect segue. "Well," he said. "Actually, I wasn't kidding about that dinner. If you're not busy tonight, I'd love to—"

"I'm sorry, I can't." Chelsea Spencer shook her head, not meeting his eyes. That was a bad sign.

He was silent then, just driving. She didn't want to go out with him. He didn't need a rejection stamped onto his forehead. But then she glanced at him. Eye contact. It was all the encouragement he needed.

"Look, I've got all of Sunday off," he said, turning to gaze at her as he pulled up to a red light. "And if you're busy then, let me give you my phone number, and that way, if you're ever not busy, you can give *me* a call and—"

"I'm busy Sunday." She met his eyes, firmly, squarely.

Johnny was the one who had to look away as the traffic moved forward. He was about a block and a half from Chelsea's office, and he pulled into the right lane, keeping his signal on so that the cars behind him knew he was going to stop.

"I'm sorry," she said softly, and as he put the truck into park he looked over at her.

She was still watching him and she *did* look sorry. Was it the money thing? Or maybe it was the class thing. She probably came from a family who could trace their roots back before the time of the *Mayflower*. Johnny's father, however, was a first-generation American, paternity unknown.

Or maybe it was just an unspoken rule. Girls from Brookline didn't date guys from his part of town. But maybe someday she'd decide to break the rules.

He reached alongside the seat for his clipboard and the pen that was attached. "Let me give you my number—"

Chelsea was shaking her head. "I don't think so. Because on Sunday—"

"Take it anyway," he said, writing his home number on a scrap of paper. " 'Cause you never know, you know?"

" . . . I'm getting married."

Johnny looked up. She was still looking at him, her blue eyes apologetic. "Married," he repeated.

She nodded. "On Sunday."

"*This* Sunday?"

Another nod.

He looked out the window. "Oh." He put down the clipboard, glancing over at her. "I'm sorry. I didn't mean to make you uncomfortable..."

"And I didn't mean to make *you* uncomfortable." She slipped out of the truck. "Don't forget to make that police report."

"I won't."

"Thanks again." She gave him one last smile and shut the door.

"Hey, Chelsea."

She pulled herself up on the running board and looked in the open window.

"This guy you're marrying on Sunday..."

"Emilio Santangelo," she said.

Emilio Santangelo. It was as Italian-American a name as Giovanni Anziano. It could have been him. He, Johnny Anziano, could have been standing at that altar come Sunday morning.

Not that he wanted to marry Chelsea Spencer. He just wanted a date or two. Or twelve. Or thirty...And hell, if she was going to marry some guy named Santangelo, she would've had no problem going on a date with an Anziano. It was his tough luck, though. He was too damn late.

"Tell Emilio congratulations for me," Johnny told her. "Tell him he's one hell of a lucky guy."

Chelsea smiled at him. "Thanks, John. For everything."

# TWO

"Hi, Chels. It's me, 'Milio. It's really important that you call me back. It doesn't matter what time it is here in Rome, just *call me*."

*Beep.*

"Chelsea, it's Emilio again. There's something wrong with your phone at home and I can't get through. As soon as you get this message, call me. Day or night."

*Beep.*

"Chelsea. Where are you? If you're in the office, pick up the phone."

*Beep.*

"Chelsea, It's three in the morning here, and I can't put this off any longer. I didn't want to leave this on your answering machine, but...I can't marry you. I can't do it—I'm sorry. I've canceled my plane ticket. I'm not coming on Saturday. I met a woman, Chels. I swear to God, I didn't mean for this to happen, but...I fell in love. I know you're probably never going to talk to me again, but call me, all right? Just...call me."

Chelsea sat at her desk, pressing the replay button on her answering machine and playing the series of messages from Emilio again and again.

Love. Her fiancé had gone and fallen in love.

With her digital answering-machine system, his smooth, faintly Italian-accented voice sounded as if he were standing right there, with her in her office.

He wasn't coming on Saturday. He wasn't going to marry her.

Moira O'Brien stood in the doorway, silently listening as Chelsea played Emilio's last message for a third time.

"Breach of promise," Chelsea said as her best friend and business partner came in to sit down across from her desk. "This was more than a marriage—this was a business proposition. He's reneging. I can't believe it."

"So sue the son-of-a-bitch."

"Moira, he's my friend. I can't sue him."

"You wanna bet?" Moira reached for the telephone. "My brother's a lawyer. Let me give him a call—"

"I'm not going to sue Emilio." Chelsea pulled the telephone out of reach. "But the next time I see him, you better believe I'm going to make him crawl to beg forgiveness." She put her head down on the desk with a thump. "Oh, Moira, what are we going to do?"

"About the bank loan?"

Chelsea lifted her head to meet her friend's worried eyes. "No, about the five hundred and fifty-seven shrimp cocktails that will go to waste—*Yes,* about the bank loan. The first payment is due three weeks from Monday. If I don't get married on Sunday, I don't get my hands on the money from my trust fund."

"You've looked at the terms of your grandfather's will?" Moira asked. "There're no loopholes?"

Chelsea opened the file drawer of her desk and

pulled out a folder. She took the photocopied page that was clipped to the inside cover and passed it across the desk to her friend.

"Chelsea Jasmine Spencer to receive the first payment of funds from a trust to the amount of two hundred and fifty thousand dollars, plus all interest accrued, upon the first business day following the return from a honeymoon, preceded by her wedding." Chelsea recited the words she knew by heart. "Additional terms regarding release of funds to be revealed at that time."

Moira chewed on her lower lip. "Additional terms?"

"Knowing sweet, rich, manipulative, *controlling* old Grandpa, it could be anything," Chelsea told her. "I might have to wear a clown suit to work for the next five weeks." She took the paper back from Moira and returned the file to its place. "Of course, now I'll never know."

"Your mother's going to have a heart attack when you tell her the wedding's off. She's going to die."

"Or worse yet," Chelsea said wickedly, "she'll live, and spend the rest of her life reminding me how *I* embarrassed *her* by being jilted three days before my wedding day."

"Jilted. That implies a certain emotional attachment, doesn't it? You don't love Emilio and he doesn't love you. Maybe this is for the best."

"Moira, if I don't get my hands on that money...Let me see. How can I put this delicately? How about: We're *screwed*!" She gestured at the room around them. "If we don't come up with that loan payment, this whole business gets flushed."

"You could borrow the money from your dad. Or one of your brothers."

"I could also sell my soul to Satan," Chelsea retorted, pushing her chair back from her desk and starting to pace.

Moira ran her fingers through her mass of red curls, making them even wilder than ever. "I know getting your family involved in Spencer/O'Brien Software is the last thing you want to do..."

"If I let them lend me money, they'll be breathing down my neck," Chelsea said. "Every single little tiny minute obscure move I make will be criticized. 'Are you sure you want to do that, sweetie?' 'Why not try it *this* way instead, Chelsea-bean?

That's the way *I* did it, kitten, and it worked for me.'"

"...but it's better than bankruptcy, isn't it?"

"No."

"Yes, it is."

"No, it's not. Believe me, you've never been called 'Chelsea-bean.' In front of a client." Chelsea turned to look at Moira, her eyes narrowing. "Your brother Edward's not married, is he?"

Moira knew exactly where this was leading. "No, but he's living with someone."

"Your older brother—Ron? He's the lawyer, right?"

"Chelsea, as your maid of honor, I have to advise you to cancel the wedding. This isn't like some daytime soap opera where one of the actors calls in sick." Moira assumed a television announcer's ultrasmooth voice. "'Today, playing the part of Chelsea's groom will be Moira's brother Ron.'"

Chelsea stopped pacing. "Do you think he'd do it?"

"Not a chance. He's married. I was just using him as an example of your insanity—"

"What about your younger brother?"

"Jimmy? He's thirteen."

But Chelsea had already dismissed him. "He's also a redhead. I need to find someone who looks Italian. My parents haven't met Emilio, and if I can find someone who looks—" She broke off, staring out the plate-glass window onto the street below. A white truck was driving past, bouncing and clattering as its wheels hit a pothole. "Giovanni Anziano," she whispered.

"Who?"

Chelsea turned to face Moira. "If you were a truck driver, probably earning just a little over minimum wage, and someone offered you, say, seventy-five thousand dollars to get married, take a free trip to the Virgin Islands, and then get the marriage annulled, would you do it?"

"Depends who I'd have to marry. Orlando Bloom, yes. Homer Simpson, no way. Who's Giovanni What's-his-name?"

"Anziano. He's the man who got my purse away from those kids." Chelsea picked up the phone and dialed information. "He's the man who's going to save my butt again— Hello? Boston, please. I'd like the number for Meals on Wheels."

———

"See you tomorrow, Mr. Gruber! Remember, medium high for five minutes in the microwave."

"All right, Martin," came the elderly man's quavering reply. "Don't let the cat out when you open the door."

"I won't." He wouldn't let the cat out because the cat—as well as Albert Gruber's son Martin— had been gone for nearly forty years. "And it's Johnny, remember? Johnny Anziano from Meals on Wheels. Catch you later, Mr. G, all right?"

Johnny locked the door behind him. He rolled his shoulders and neck as he took the stairs down from Mr. Gruber's fourth-floor apartment. The old man was slipping further into the past. It used to be his moments of confusion were few and far between, but lately, Mr. Gruber had been calling him "Martin" more often.

Johnny stepped out onto the sidewalk. Today had been a particularly bad day for Mr. Gruber. There was no way the old guy was going to remember to heat up that plate of food in the microwave come dinnertime. Johnny was going to have to call him from the restaurant's office and remind him and—

Chelsea Spencer was leaning up against his truck.

Johnny stopped short, doing a quick double take. Yes, that was definitely his truck. There were no other Meals on Wheels trucks parked on this street. And yes, that was definitely Chelsea Spencer. Her blond hair was pulled back into a French braid and she was wearing some kind of dark business suit with wide-legged pants and a jacket that managed to be both mannishly cut and thoroughly feminine. Or maybe it was the fact that Chelsea was wearing it that made it seem so feminine.

She straightened up as she caught sight of him, obviously waiting for him.

"Hi, John. Remember me?" She looked slightly self-conscious, slightly nervous. "Chelsea Spencer."

Johnny had to laugh. Did he remember her? It was a ludicrous question. "What are you doing here?"

He looked around at the crumbling brownstone apartment buildings, at the littered sidewalks, at the bent and fading street sign. Yes, this was definitely one of the crummiest streets in one of the crummiest parts of town. He looked again and

Chelsea Spencer was still standing next to his truck, impossibly out of place.

"Are you all right?" he asked.

She nodded, another flash of something faintly shy and sweet in her blue eyes. "You're...taller than I remembered."

Her eyes lingered on the front of his T-shirt, and he glanced down, suddenly panicked that he was wearing another embarrassing slogan across his chest. But no. Today he was a walking billboard for athletic shoes. JUST DO IT, the white letters on his shirt proclaimed.

Chelsea tried to hide a smile, meeting his eyes only briefly, and he knew without a doubt that she was remembering the words he had been wearing the last time they met. *I'm too sexy for my shirt.* She was going to remember *that* until the end of time. No doubt he'd made one hell of a first impression.

"I wanted to talk to you about something, and the Meals on Wheels office wouldn't give out your phone number. It's kind of urgent, so instead of leaving you a message, I talked them into telling me your route. I was starting to worry this wasn't really your truck," she added. "You were gone an awfully long time."

Johnny nodded. "Mr. Gruber's my last delivery of the morning. Sometimes he needs a little extra attention. Today I played a couple of games of cards with him and helped him repot a plant. But if I'd known you were waiting..."

"I didn't mind waiting." She shifted her weight and cleared her throat and jammed her hands into the pockets of her jacket. She was definitely nervous and Johnny was intrigued. "If you're done for the day...Do you have to get the truck right back? Or can you take some time to talk?"

His curiosity kicked into overdrive. "What, did they find the kids who snatched your purse? You need me to testify or something?"

She shook her head no. "I noticed there's a coffee shop just around the corner. Would you mind if we sat down and talked?"

"Sure," he said. "That'd be great."

Johnny forced himself to be cool. She'd asked him to have a cup of coffee. So what? It wasn't like it was a date or anything—after all, the lady was getting married in just a few short days.

"Have you ever been married?" she asked,

glancing up at him as they walked down the cracked and uneven sidewalk.

"No. Have you?"

She shook her head again. "No. So you're not separated, or waiting for a divorce to come through or something like that?"

She was watching him closely, as if his answer were very important.

"Nope."

"No steady girlfriend? No significant other?"

Johnny stopped walking, suddenly realizing where this line of questioning was leading. "You're going to set me up, aren't you?" he guessed. "You have some friend who needs a date for your wedding, right?"

Chelsea hesitated, chewing slightly on her lower lip. "Well, sort of ... You see ..."

She was gazing up at him, her blue eyes so wide that she looked about twelve years old. He could drown in those eyes, Johnny realized. He could just fall right in and never come back out.

She took a deep breath and gave him a somewhat tentative smile. "You see, *I* need a date for my wedding."

He stared at her, convinced he'd misunderstood. "You need a *what*?"

"Groom," she said. "I need a groom. My fiancé canceled on me and—"

"He *canceled* on you?" Johnny's voice went up a full octave in shock. "You mean, he *ditched* you? *You*?"

She smiled very slightly. "I appreciate your disbelief, but yeah, he ditched me. Three days before the wedding."

"What kind of fool is he, anyway?"

"The kind of fool who's in love with someone else," she said.

"Whoa. That must've hurt."

"No, it's not that bad, really. The marriage was just a business arrangement, anyway. I needed a husband, and Emilio wanted a green card, and..." She shrugged. "It hurt, but not in the way you mean because, well, I wasn't in love with him."

Johnny couldn't believe what he was hearing. "You needed a husband badly enough to marry someone you didn't love?"

"I still need a husband," she told him quietly.

He gazed back at her. He heard her words. He understood them. He just couldn't believe them.

"What are you telling me, Chelsea?" He knew. He just had to have it spelled out. He wanted to hear it from her own lips.

"I'm not telling, I'm asking," she said. She took a deep breath and squared her shoulders. "John, I'm asking you to marry me on Sunday."

# THREE

"*This Sunday?*" Johnny asked, as if that were the incomprehensibly insane part of her crazy request.

Chelsea nodded, gazing up at him. She'd shocked him. Utterly. She could see his surprise clearly in his eyes—for once they were open wide. He was floored, and she couldn't blame him. If a virtual stranger had approached her and asked her in all seriousness to marry him, she'd long ago have been running as fast as she could in the opposite direction.

So far Giovanni Anziano wasn't running.

She glanced over her shoulder at the door to the

coffee shop. "Can we go inside? I'd like to explain."

He was noticeably silent as he followed her into the tiny restaurant, but at least he was following her.

There was a booth free by the window, and Chelsea slid onto one of the vinyl banquettes. Johnny sat down across from her. Some of the shock in his eyes had changed to wariness. He was willing to hear her out, but she knew he was far from giving her a yes.

"Why do you need a husband?" he asked. "Are you in trouble? Are you going to have a baby?"

It was funny, but Chelsea had the feeling that if she said yes, he'd seriously consider helping her out and marrying her so that her baby would have a name. Or maybe it wasn't funny. After all, Giovanni Anziano was the kind of man who voluntarily spent several mornings each week delivering food for Meals on Wheels. He wasn't paid for driving that white truck—she had learned that after talking to the receptionist at the charity organization. And he was the kind of man who took the time from his busy schedule to play a game or two of cards with one of the lonely old men on his route.

"I'm not pregnant," she said. "I'm in a different kind of trouble. I'm in kind of a financial bind."

He had been watching her intently, but now he glanced up. A waitress had come to their table.

"I'll have a coffee," he said. "Cream and sugar." He looked at Chelsea. "You too?"

"Herbal tea, please."

The waitress shook her head. "Don't have it. Only regular tea or coffee."

"Then just a pot of hot water with lemon, please." Chelsea glanced at Johnny as the waitress left. "I don't do caffeine."

"Too bad. I make a mean espresso."

Chelsea had to look away. There was something highly volatile that seemed to spark and burst into flames every time she so much as glanced into this man's eyes. That wasn't good. She wasn't looking for a sexual playmate—she was looking for a business partner.

But this guy was so damned attractive, it was hard to keep her mind on business.

Still, now that Emilio had backed out, too attractive or not, John Anziano was the only man around. He was her only hope.

"My college roommate and I started our own

business last year," she explained. "Computer software. Moira—she's my friend—is a programmer, too, and we figured why work for someone else when we could work for ourselves. But we underestimated our start-up expenses and reached a point a few months ago where we either had to call it quits and lose everything or get creative in our financing."

The waitress returned with their order, and Chelsea poured steaming-hot water from a tiny, silver-colored teapot into her mug. John added cream and sugar to his coffee as she continued.

"We streamlined, moving into that office in a lower-rent part of town. We also got creative with our assets. You see, when my grandfather died a few years ago, he left money in trust for all of his grandchildren. But according to his will, we can't get our hands on that money until we're legally wed."

She glanced across the table and into Johnny's chocolate-brown eyes. Chocolate was one of the few things that she truly missed since she'd cut sugar out of her diet several years ago.

"So you're getting married in order to get your hands on your inheritance," he said.

She shielded her slice of lemon with one hand as she squeezed the juice into her mug of hot water. "It's a little more complicated than that," she admitted. "After Emilio agreed to marry me, I went to a bank and got a loan—kind of an advance on the money I'd be receiving from the trust fund. I have to start making those loan payments in a few weeks, and the business isn't up to bringing in that kind of money yet, so..."

"Why not just borrow the money to repay the loan?"

She took a sip of her hot water and lemon. "Do you know someone who'll lend me over two hundred and fifty thousand dollars, interest-free?" she asked.

He nearly dropped his coffee mug. "*That's* how much you need to pay back the loan?"

"No, but that's how much I'll get from my inheritance. I was intending to sink that money into the business." She gazed at him. "I *need* to get married. And not just for the money. This whole thing has gotten bigger than I imagined. The ceremony, the reception—I have relatives already arriving from out of town. I can't cancel now."

"Chelsea, you know, it happens sometimes. It's really not that big a deal. People call weddings off."

"Yeah, well, Spencers aren't 'people.' Spencers are above making such nasty little messes with their lives. Or so I'm told."

"Emilio's the one to blame. He's the one who walked. You had no control over his actions."

"I should have—at least that's what my parents will say. I should have made certain that a prize catch like Emilio Santangelo didn't get away. After all, he's in a power position at one of the biggest financial institutions in Rome—not to mention the fact that he's descended from royalty. That went over really well with Mother and Daddy."

"He is?"

"See, even *you're* impressed. You can bet I'll be lectured for years on how it was *my* mistake that I let him get away. The same way I've been lectured for the past seven years on what a mistake it was not to get married right out of college. My parents believe a woman isn't complete without a husband. Forget your degrees and all those years of studying—you can become the CEO of General Motors, and you still won't be whole until you find a man and get married. After that you can fool around with your little career all you want—as long as it doesn't get in the way of your devotion to your beloved lord and master."

Johnny was laughing at her vehemence.

Chelsea sat back in her seat, giving him a rueful smile. "Sorry. I'm a little irate about the whole thing. They've been pressuring me to get married for close to an eternity now. It gets old after a while. If it was up to me, I'd never get married. I'm quite complete on my own, thank you very much."

"So you didn't tell your parents that you and Emilio were only tying the knot to get the money," Johnny said.

"No, I didn't. I just told them I was finally getting married and let them take it from there. And they took it and ran. The reception is going to be huge. My parents have a guest list of nearly six hundred people."

Johnny whistled. "Holy God, who's catering that?"

"I don't know. I don't *care*." She gazed down at her mug and sighed. "I just wanted it to be over." She glanced up at him. "Here's my offer: I'll give you seventy-five thousand dollars and a trip to the Virgin Islands if you show up at the church on Sunday and pretend to be Emilio. After the reception, you'll fly out to Vegas with me and we'll get married for real. We'll go from there to St. Thomas, spend a few days at the beach, then show up at the lawyer's office with our marriage certificate in hand. We'll get the money, and in a few days—a week or two at the most—we'll quietly get the marriage annulled."

He took a long sip of his coffee, watching her over the rim of his mug. When he put the mug down, he laughed in disbelief. "This is definitely one of the more bizarre days of my life."

"I know it sounds crazy, but, John, I really need your help."

"You don't know me. What if I'm some kind of weirdo?"

"You work for Meals on Wheels. Little old ladies open their doors for you, remember?"

"Explain to me the part about Vegas again," he said. "I'm not sure I follow that. We get married *twice*?"

Chelsea felt a burst of hope. Was he actually considering doing this? She tried to keep her voice even and matter-of-fact. "Vegas is to make it legal. I've already checked into it—there's no way we can get a Massachusetts marriage license by this coming Sunday."

He nodded slowly. "Seventy-five K, huh?"

"Yes." She held her breath. She could almost see the wheels turning in Johnny's head. God, what she would have given to know what he was thinking.

"And a honeymoon in St. Thomas too? How many days?"

"Four days, three nights." She crossed her fingers under the table, making a wish. Please, please, *please,* say yes.

"I've got some time off coming to me," he said, thinking aloud. "Rudy, my boss, isn't going to like me springing it on him with hardly any notice, but..."

"Does this mean...?" she whispered, hardly daring to hope.

He smiled. "If we're going to do this, we oughta do it right, don't you think?" He reached across the table and took her hand, lacing their fingers together. "Chelsea Spencer, will you marry me—for a week or two?"

Chelsea felt a rush of tears fill her eyes. His hands were big and warm and they seemed to engulf hers completely. It was an odd sensation. "Yes," she said. She smiled at him across the table, blinking back her tears. "Thank you, John, so very much."

This was one crazy idea.

Of course, Johnny had had some experience with crazy ideas in the past. He'd pulled some particularly insane stunts before—like hopping aboard the red-eye to Paris with a friend from the Culinary Institute simply to settle an argument over whether it was lovage or cilantro that master chef Donatien Solange of the Hotel Cartier used in his world-famous lemon-lime chicken.

It was lovage.

Johnny had been right. He'd won the argument, but the round-trip ticket had cost him all of his second-semester spending money.

He squeezed his VW Bug into a half of a parking spot on Boylston Street, wondering what this latest crazy idea was going to cost him.

He was marrying Chelsea Spencer on Sunday. The thought still made him laugh out loud. It was one hell of a first date, and one amazingly crazy idea.

Supposedly it was going to cost him nothing. Supposedly he was going to get seventy-five bills gigundo for the pleasure of giving the lovely Ms. Spencer his name—albeit only temporarily. But if there was one thing he'd learned so far in life along with how to make a near-perfect crêpe, it was that crazy ideas *always* had hefty price tags.

But how could he turn down seventy-five grand? The money would put him a year and a half closer to owning his own restaurant. And how could he not notice those tears of gratitude that had flooded Chelsea's crystal-blue eyes when he'd told her he'd help her out? And how could he not think about the fact that he'd be flying to some Caribbean paradise to share the honeymoon suite for three hot, tropical nights with a lady who made his blood pressure rise?

The possibilities were endless and extremely tantalizing.

He got out of his car, glancing again at the address Chelsea had scrawled on the back of one of her business cards. Her attorney's office. It was a Newbury Street address—just a few blocks away.

He picked up his pace as the first fat drops of rain began to fall.

Newbury Street was made up of graceful old brownstones, some elegantly restored, but some renovated with gleaming metal and shining glass. It was a jangling mixture of old and new, a vibrant neighborhood filled with trendy restaurants, up-scale fashion boutiques, and avant-garde record and CD stores. Offices and condos were nestled in among the shops, and on the other side of the heavy wooden front doors, those offices tended to be either crumbling and slightly seedy or gor-geously preserved.

Johnny took the stairs up to the attorney's building, betting he was going to see an office that was gorgeously preserved.

He wasn't disappointed.

The reception area was something out of an old movie. The wood trim around the windows and doors gleamed. The ceilings were high, and pol-ished brass gas fixtures were still in place.

An elegant-looking receptionist was sitting be-hind an enormous oak desk, gazing at him over the top of a pair of half glasses. "Are you here to pick up the delivery?"

Johnny had to laugh. Figures he'd be mistaken for the hired help. "No. Actually, I'm here to see Tim von Reuter."

"Really?" She gave him a very pointed once-over, lingering disapprovingly on his shoulder-length hair, his faded jeans, and his rain-spotted T-shirt.

He returned her gaze just as steadily, feeling his temper start to rise. "Yes, really."

"I'm sorry, you don't seem to be in *Mister* von Reuter's book. You'll have to call for an appointment. Good day." She turned away from him.

Johnny knocked on her desk to get her attention. "Hate to disappoint you, lady, but I do have an appointment. One o'clock. You can tell Mr. von Reuter that *Mister* Anziano is here to see him."

"John. Good, you made it."

He turned to see Chelsea coming into the outer office, closing the door behind her.

His fiancée.

Nobody would mistake her for a delivery person.

She was still wearing the same dark suit she'd had on this morning, and she still looked like about a million very elegant bucks. He forgot all about the snob lady behind the desk as Chelsea set her umbrella in a brass stand and smiled at him. It was a sweet smile, almost shy. She met his eyes only briefly as she set her enormous purse on a chair and shrugged out of her raincoat. "I was half-afraid you wouldn't come."

"I said I'd be here."

"John, it's okay if you want to change your mind—"

"Do *you* want to change your mind?"

"*No!*" She looked up at him then, her blue eyes wide. She glanced at the receptionist and lowered her voice. "I just...I know you must be having second thoughts and doubts, so..."

"I definitely have some questions to ask the lawyer before I sign anything," Johnny said evenly.

She took a deep breath and gave him a somewhat wobbly smile. "Then let's do it. Let's talk to Tim." She turned to the receptionist. "Mrs. Mert, will you please tell Mr. von Reuter that we're here."

"We?" the lady asked icily, with another grim look at Johnny.

"My fiancé and I," Chelsea said, with a hint of that same chill in her voice. "We're here to sign a prenuptial agreement."

Mrs. Mert stood up and moved silently down a corridor with one last disapproving look back at Johnny.

"Is that a class you can take in private school?" Johnny asked. "You know, Chilly Disapproval 101? She's definitely a master, but you're not so bad at it yourself."

"Oh, God, please don't compare me to Mrs. Mert. She wasn't exactly hired for her tolerance."

"No kidding. I think she likes me about as much as she likes getting a piece of bubble gum stuck on the bottom of her shoe."

She smiled at him. "The gum she can take care of with some ice and a putty knife. You look a little bit more difficult to get rid of."

"Why, because I'm not wearing a business suit and a noose—I mean, tie—around my neck?"

"That's part of it." Chelsea gazed at him. "But I think it's mostly your hair," she said.

"My *hair*?"

"Wait a sec." She sat down and dug to the bottom of her purse, coming up with a ponytail holder. "Try this."

He sat down next to her. "It's more than my hair. It's the 'us versus them' theory. Mrs. Mert thinks she's 'us,' and I'm definitely 'them.' You're 'us,' too, although your status is shaky now that you've been seen with me."

Chelsea studied him almost pensively as he raked his hair back with his fingers, gathering it into a ponytail. "You're probably right," she said. "People like Mrs. Mert feel threatened by people like you."

"People like me." Did she mean people in his tax bracket, or people who were born in a crummy part of town with a less-than-pure pedigree?

"People like you," Chelsea repeated, "who are too sexy for their shirts." She was doing her best not to smile, but she couldn't hide the sparkling amusement in her eyes.

"Damn," he said with a laugh. "You're never going to let me live that down."

"You know what they say about first impressions."

"Let's see, if I remember correctly, I wrestled your handbag away from muggers, staring down a pretty nasty-looking switchblade knife in the process, *and* okay, yes, I *was* wearing a dumb T-shirt. But somehow you only seem to remember the shirt part."

"Some things just stand out above the rest." She grinned at him. "I heard that song on the radio just about an hour ago, and it occurred to me that we should use it for our first dance at the reception."

"Your parents would *love* that." Dance. They were going to have to dance at the reception. He would have to hold her in his arms and—

"I would ask the band to play an instrumental version—my parents would never know."

"Whoa, you're not kidding, are you?"

She just smiled at him. "We need to get you fitted for a tuxedo," she said. "And do you happen to know your ring size?"

"Ring size? Not a chance. But I already have a tux."

"Black shoes?"

"Got 'em. Italian leather—Emilio would approve."

She pointed to his ponytail. "That's definitely the way an Italian investment banker would wear his hair. It's very high finance."

"Are you sure I don't need a scrunchee with dollar signs on it or something?"

"No scrunchees. Unless they're Italian leather." She paused. "John, it's occurred to me that you may not know much about banking and the stock market and all that. I mean, I don't even know where you work—besides Meals on Wheels."

"I work at Lumière's—it's a restaurant downtown." He could see from her eyes that she didn't recognize the name. He could also see that she was not impressed. Most people weren't—until they tasted his cooking. "And you're right," he said. "The most that I know about banking is that my savings account doesn't make nearly enough interest anymore. And as far as investments go, right now my sole investment is a two-dollar quick-pick lottery ticket I've got for next Wednesday's drawing."

"I'm going to have Emilio give you a call," Chelsea decided. "He can give you a crash course in international banking."

"It's not necessary."

"Oh, yes, it is. What are you going to do when my father starts asking you questions about the Italian economy?"

"I'll do this." Johnny leaned forward slightly, bringing his finger up to his lips in a gesture of silence. He spoke with a faintly foreign-sounding accent. "Shhh. Today is a day of pleasure and celebration, not business. We will talk of such things another time."

Her graceful lips quirked upward in a smile and she snorted, trying not to laugh. "I hate to break it to you, but you sound like Mr. Roarke from *Fantasy Island*."

He gave her a mock scowl. "No, I don't. I sound like Emilio."

"Hmmm. Do you speak any Italian?"

Johnny rubbed his chin. "Only a few phrases. And *definitely* nothing I can toss out at your wedding reception, believe me."

She began searching for something in her purse, glancing at him out of the corner of her eye. "I guess Mr. Roarke will have to do."

Johnny stretched his legs out in front of him and crossed his ankles. "So which of my tuxes do you want me to wear on Sunday? The light blue polyester or the maroon velvet?"

The look on her face was priceless. She actually believed he was serious.

"I've got this pink ruffled shirt that goes great with either of 'em...." he continued, unable to keep from smiling at her look of total horror. "Chelsea, I'm kidding. Black. My tuxedo is black.

I was just getting back at you for saying I sounded like a character from a bad TV show."

"But I loved that show. I adored Mr. Roarke.... Until he turned into Khan and killed Mr. Spock in *Star Trek II*." She paused. "You did say your tuxedo is black, right?"

"Black and only a year old. Right in fashion. Designer label. Fits like a glove. Women faint when I wear it in public."

"I'll bet." She found whatever she was looking for in her purse, pulled it free, and handed it to him. "Here, Don Giovanni, try this on for size."

It was a jeweler's box, covered with soft black velvet. It was a ring box. Johnny popped it open, and there, inside, was a gleaming golden band. He looked up at Chelsea, suddenly subdued. She, too, had fallen silent.

This was a wedding ring. An age-old symbol of commitment and love. But Chelsea was joining him in holy matrimony on Sunday, and neither of them was expecting either.

"I tried to guess your size," she said softly.

The ring was gorgeous in its simplicity. Johnny ran one finger lightly over it, but when he pulled it from the box he fumbled and dropped it on the plush carpeting.

Chelsea bent over and picked it up. "Here," she said, reaching for his hand.

She slid the ring onto his finger.

It seemed far too intimate an act. Far too personal for two people who barely knew each other. Chelsea looked up into his eyes, and for Johnny, time seemed to stand still.

"It fits," she whispered, still holding his hand.

It did fit. Snugly. Perfectly. About as perfectly as her hand fit in his.

"Good guess," he said. His voice sounded odd too. Breathless.

"Mr. von Reuter will see you now," Mrs. Mert announced, appearing suddenly, like a specter from the mist.

Chelsea jumped and dropped Johnny's hand as if he'd burned her.

Johnny looked down at the ring he was wearing on his left hand.

Married.

On Sunday, he was going to get married. He should be searching his soul, questioning the moral implications of so casually entering into one of the holy sacraments. He was, after all, at least half-Catholic.

But instead, all he could think was how much he couldn't wait to kiss the bride.

# FOUR

CHELSEA LIKED HIM. She honestly liked Johnny Anziano.

He was charming and smart, and he had a good sense of humor, thank God. And he certainly wasn't difficult to look at, that much was for sure. As if he felt her watching him, he glanced in her direction and she quickly looked away.

She found Johnny much too attractive. This was a huge mistake. How on earth was she going to live with this man for a week or two without getting in too deep?

Control. Willpower. She took a deep breath. She could do it. She was going to *have* to do it.

Tim von Reuter droned on, explaining the terms of the prenuptial agreement as Johnny read over the documents.

"I have a question," he said in his smoky voice when Von Reuter stopped for a breath. God, even his voice had the power to send shivers up and down her spine.

This had to stop. Johnny Anziano was just a man. She'd had working relationships with men before, with absolutely no shivers up or down any part of her anatomy.

Johnny glanced at Chelsea again. "About the annulment... You mention annulment as a means of ending the marriage, but... Clue me in here, Tim. If annulment is so much easier and faster, why does anyone bother with divorce?"

Von Reuter cleared his throat. "We have connections to a judge who will grant unopposed annulments provided the marriage has not been consummated. Most marriages are consummated."

Chelsea looked up and met Johnny's gaze. Instant fire. He didn't smile this time—was it possible, he, too, couldn't manage to move any of his muscles at all?

Somehow she managed to pull her gaze away and she heard him shift in his chair as if he, too, had suddenly been freed.

Her lawyer leaned toward Johnny. "This marriage is going to be a business partnership. You do understand that you're going to be married in name only?"

Johnny nodded. "I understand that. But..." He paused, as if searching for the right words. "What if...?" He cleared his throat. "I'm not saying that it's going to happen, but if something does happen, I mean..." He was embarrassed, but this was clearly important enough for him to plow on through. "If something happens of, um, an intimate nature between Chelsea and me, then we'll have to go through the whole divorce procedure, is that what you're saying?"

"Nothing's going to happen." Chelsea wished she felt as confident as she sounded.

Von Reuter put in his two cents. "Such *an... event* would be difficult to prove, if you know what I'm saying."

"In other words, if we slipped and 'accidentally'

had sex—if such a thing is possible—we could lie about it under oath when it comes time to end the marriage?" Chelsea snorted and shook her head. "That's unacceptable. I won't do that." She turned to Johnny. "If a sexual relationship is an important part of what you're hoping to get out of this deal, you may as well walk out the door right now."

God, were they actually sitting here in her lawyer's office discussing *sex*? Chelsea could hardly breathe.

Johnny was sitting back in his seat, obviously going nowhere as he gave her one of his extremely potent smiles. "It's no big deal. I was just wondering how many cold showers I'd have to take over the next few weeks."

"As many as you need," she told him. But how many would *she* need? As many as it took, she decided grimly. There was no way she was putting this deal in jeopardy.

She made a mental note to take a vast amount of work with her to St. Thomas. And she'd call the hotel again this afternoon to be absolutely certain that the connecting rooms she'd reserved had a door with a working lock between them. Control was always easier when temptation was reduced.

Johnny sat forward, reaching for a pen, and glancing once more in her direction, he signed the agreement.

Chelsea felt giddy as the document was passed to her. "I don't have your card," she said to Johnny, thinking aloud as she initialed the pages and added her signature to the bottom.

"I don't have a card," Johnny told her as they both shook Von Reuter's hand and rose to leave the room.

"Do you have a phone number?" she asked, opening her appointment book to the back as Tim walked them out to the reception area. She jotted down the numbers Johnny gave her for both home and work. "The wedding's at noon on Sunday at the First Congregational Church. Do you have a fax at work? I can send you directions...."

"I'll see you both on Sunday," Von Reuter said, disappearing toward his office.

Johnny held the door to the street open for her. "I know where the church is."

It was raining in earnest now, and Chelsea slipped on her raincoat and opened her umbrella. It seemed so odd. She and this stranger had just signed a marriage agreement. She and this stranger were going to be married in a matter of days....

And the marriage would be annulled in a matter of days after that, she reminded herself.

"There's a rehearsal and a dinner scheduled for Saturday evening." Chelsea held the umbrella up high enough so he could stand underneath it too. What a mistake. Now he was standing *much* too close. Whatever the faint cologne was he was wearing, it should have been illegal. It was impossibly enticing. "But I know that you have to work."

"There's no way I can get that time," he apologized. She could feel his body heat even though they weren't quite touching. "My boss nearly had a heart attack when I told him I needed a few days off after the wedding."

"It's probably better this way," she said, her mouth remarkably dry. She gazed out at the street, afraid to look up into his eyes. He was so tall and so...close. She tried to sound casual, matter-of-fact. "I'll cancel the rehearsal and the dinner and we'll just...wing it on Sunday. Just be ready for the minister to call you Emilio, all right? We'll use your real name in Vegas. Oh, do you have a copy of your birth certificate?"

Johnny nodded. "Yeah. I'll bring it. Look, can I give you a lift somewhere? My car's right around the corner."

"No. Thank you. I'm heading all the way out to Brookline. It's out of your way—I'll just catch a cab."

"It's not that big a deal."

"No, I don't want to make you late for work." What she really didn't want was to spend a fifteen-minute ride through heavy traffic sitting next to Johnny in his car. With the rain drumming on the roof and the windows steaming up, it would be far too close quarters.

"How about we get together for lunch tomorrow?" he asked.

"Tomorrow..." She let him take hold of the umbrella as she flipped open her book, already knowing what was written there. "No, I'm sorry. I'm doing lunch with my parents."

"Saturday?"

Chelsea shook her head, grateful that she had another excuse. "My mother's made me promise her the entire day," she told him. God knows she'd be spending enough time with him immediately after the wedding. Why start testing her willpower any sooner?

"I guess I'll see you Sunday, then."

"Call me if you're going to be late, or... something."

"I won't be late."

She looked up into his eyes and found him smiling at her.

"Really," he said again. "I won't be late."

His gaze flickered down to her mouth, but when he leaned forward, he kissed her gently on the cheek.

Chelsea's heart was drumming in her chest. This was insane. This was totally crazy. How was it possible that one little chaste kiss on the cheek could make her feel as if she were going to explode?

Johnny stepped out from underneath the umbrella, pressing the handle into her hands. She almost dropped it.

Control. Willpower.

Chelsea forced her mouth up into a friendly smile, forced herself to turn and walk toward the street, forced herself to lift a hand to beckon to one of the cabs that were racing by.

She could feel him watching as a cab jolted to a stop beside her. He was still standing there as she got in and the cab pulled away. She let herself sag back against the seat.

Control. Willpower. Something told her this was going to be her mantra over the next week.

"I remembered what it was that I didn't tell you."

Johnny gazed blearily at the red numbers of the digital clock on his bedside table: 3:40 A.M. "Chelsea?" he said into the phone.

"Yeah, it's me. I know I probably woke you, but all I could think about was what if I waited until the morning to call, and then you weren't home and..." He heard her draw in a deep breath. "I'm sorry, John. God, I'm really losing it. Please, will you do me a favor and call me first thing in the morning? It's really important."

He reached over and turned on the light, squinting in the sudden brightness. "No, it's all right," he said, running his hand over his eyes and the roughness of his cheeks and chin. "I haven't been asleep for that long. I only get home from work at twelve-thirty on a Friday, and then I'm usually too wired to go right to bed. And tonight I was bouncing off the walls. Too much coffee, probably." Tonight he'd stared at the ceiling for a solid hour after he'd gotten into bed, thinking about the fact that he was getting *married* day after tomorrow. "What's up?"

"Can you really talk now? I mean, you're not busy, I mean, you don't have company?"

Johnny had to laugh. "Maybe after we get to Vegas there'll be time for us to talk—get to know each other a little bit better. And then I can tell you things about myself like, I don't do one-night stands, and that I certainly wouldn't start an affair two days before I was planning to marry someone else."

Chelsea was silent for a moment. "I'm sorry. I didn't mean to offend you."

"Hey, no offense taken—it takes more than that to offend *me*. But of course you wouldn't know that either, would you?"

"We don't know each other at all," she said quietly.

Johnny leaned back against his pillows, tucking

the phone under his chin. "So let's make a date for Vegas. Whaddaya say?"

Another pause. "Maybe it's better if we just... don't get to know each other."

"Aren't you curious about me?"

"Well, yes, but..."

He could hear rustling on her end, as if she, too, were settling back in her bed. The thought brought all sorts of incredible pictures to mind and his throat suddenly felt tight. His voice was husky when he spoke. "But what?" he asked.

"It's not like we're really getting married," she pointed out. "It's a business deal. I've done business with people I've known absolutely nothing about."

He cleared his throat. "Yeah, well, you haven't had to go on a honeymoon with *them*, have you?"

She laughed. "No, thank God."

"I'm way curious about you," he said. "I don't even know your favorite color."

"You also don't know anything about my family—and that's why I called."

"You called at three-forty in the morning in a near panic to tell me about your family? That's... interesting."

She laughed again. She had an incredibly musical laugh. Johnny closed his eyes, letting it wash over him. He wondered what she was wearing, wondered if she slept naked, the way he did. Forget about her favorite color—there was a whole hell of a lot of other things he was dying to know about this woman.

"It occurred to me that you would be arriving at the church on Sunday morning," Chelsea said, "and my entire family would be there—except for me. You won't see me until I'm walking down the aisle. I won't be there to introduce you to anyone."

Johnny forced himself to concentrate on her words. She would be walking down the aisle, coming to meet him at the altar.... "Are you going to be doing it up, you know, wearing a fancy wedding dress?"

"It's a gown," she said. "And yes. It's extravagant. I don't even want to tell you how much it cost."

"I bet you're going to look beautiful."

"I bet you say that to all of your fiancées. John, about Sunday morning..."

"I'll be there, tuxedo clean and pressed, shoes

shined, hair back in an extremely conservative ponytail."

"But I'm not supposed to see you until after the wedding, so who's going to introduce you to my parents?"

"I think maybe since I'm the groom, your father would probably take it upon himself to approach me and shake my hand."

"Yes, but he would expect my fiancé to already know my brothers' and sister's names. But I forgot to tell you, and that's why I called and woke you up."

Aha. Now it all made sense. "How many brothers?"

"Two. Michael and Troy. Michael's going to be your best man. He's the one with glasses."

"Michael. Glasses. Best man." Johnny grabbed a pen from his bedside table. There was no paper around, so he jotted the words on the side of a tissue box. "And Troy. Got it."

"Maybe you should write it down."

"I'm already a step ahead of you, pen in motion," he said. "Sisters?"

"One. Her name's Sierra."

"Like the mountains?"

"Well, that's one memory aid. She's eight months pregnant, and kind of reminiscent of a mountain range."

"I'll be sure to tell her you said that."

"Don't you dare!"

"Husband?"

"Absolutely. We don't do unwed pregnancies in our family. Sierra got married the day after she turned twenty-two. Her husband's name is Edgar Pope and you'll recognize *him* right away too. He looks just like his name."

"Big pointy hat, long robe, funny way of waving his hand?"

Chelsea laughed and he could hear her relaxing. She had obviously envisioned an incredible screwup on Sunday in which he was exposed as a fake after failing to know her family's names.

"No," she said. "Little wire glasses, receding hairline, two-thousand-dollar hand-tailored suits— although he'll probably be wearing his tuxedo. He looks kind of like a 1930s stereotype of a millionaire—without the yacht."

"Is he a millionaire?"

She snorted. "If he's not, he should be. He's the international vice-president of some Fortune 500 company, and he works about twenty-two hours a day. These days he's always flying off on business trips to Japan and Australia and Outer Mongolia. He's never home—it's a wonder Sierra managed to get pregnant at all this time. My theory is that they met for a quickie in the airport ladies' room between his flights."

Johnny nearly choked.

"This is their third demon offspring," Chelsea told him. "They come already equipped with two junior-model Popes. An Ashley and a Skippy."

"Skippy, huh?"

"His birth certificate says Edgar Pope, Junior, but his real name is Monster. Have you heard of the terrible twos?"

"Yeah."

"Monster's going for his fourth consecutive year of the terrible twos."

"I guess you don't like kids, huh?"

"I don't like what my sister has let Edgar do to her life. She's some kind of a *trophy* wife, and she won't even acknowledge it! She does *nothing* besides take care of Edgar and the kids."

"Maybe she's happy doing that."

"Maybe she's had a lobotomy and everyone forgot to tell *me*," Chelsea huffed. "Do you know that five years ago, she and Edgar were living in San Francisco? It was just after the Monster was born, and Sierra auditioned for a really fabulous semiprofessional community chorus. She was so excited about it—it was an interracial, intercultural, inter-everything group that did all kinds of music and it was a really big deal that she got in. She told me it was a chance to unite the diversity of the community through music, without homogenizing the cultural differences. She was *so* into it— she majored in both music and anthropology in college. After about three years she was elected to sit on the board of directors, which was one heck of an honor. But then two weeks later Edgar was transferred back to the Boston office. Just like that, she had to give it up."

"But that's part of being married," Johnny said. "You know—compromise."

"Exactly," Chelsea countered hotly. "Women and men get married, and the women are the ones who have to compromise. We lose our individuality and our importance along with our identity— even our names are taken away. I'm *never* getting married."

"Correct me if I'm wrong here, but aren't you getting married in less than forty-eight hours?"

"Don't remind me."

There was real trepidation in her voice. Johnny pushed himself up, resting his weight on one elbow as he held the phone closer to his ear. "You're scared about Sunday, aren't you?"

"Hell, yes. Aren't you?"

"I guess I'm a little nervous," he told her honestly. "But I'm excited too. It's funny—it's kind of like I'm taking you to a Halloween party for our first date. You're dressing up as a bride, and I'm going as a groom."

"This isn't a date—it's a business deal," she said.

She could call it a deal—he was going to call it a date.

"Have you still got your pen handy?" she asked. "Because my parents' names are Howard and Julia."

Dutifully he wrote the names down. "Got it."

"Whatever happens on Sunday," she said, and he got the feeling she was saying this as much to herself as to him, "just grit your teeth and *smile*."

# FIVE

"BREATHE," MOIRA SAID as she adjusted Chelsea's wedding veil. "Come on, Chels, in and out. Focus only on that. Oxygen into the lungs, then exhale. Atta girl."

"What if he doesn't show?" Chelsea asked. "Oh, *God*! What if he *does*?"

"He's here," Sierra announced, coming into the little room in the back of the church. "Chelsea, you never told me Emilio Santangelo was a hunk."

"I gotta get a peek at this guy." Moira went to the door and opened it a crack. "Whoa!" She turned to Chelsea in disbelief. "*This* is your truck—"

Truck driver. She'd almost said, "This is your truck driver," right in front of Chelsea's sister, who still believed that Johnny was Emilio, the investment banker from Italy.

"Sierra, will you please go and check on the flowers?" Chelsea could hear the desperation in her voice, but there was nothing she could do about it. "And run interference with Mom? She's the last thing I need right now—criticizing my makeup and hair. You know how she gets when she's tense."

"You only have about three minutes before you have to get out there," her sister warned as she closed the door behind her.

Three minutes. "All right," Chelsea said weakly. Three minutes. And then she'd have to walk down that aisle on her father's arm. It was the kind of symbolism she really despised—being "given" by one man, her father, to another, her soon-to-be husband, as if she were some sort of booty or prize.

It wasn't going to be real, she tried to tell herself. It wouldn't be legal. Johnny Anziano *wasn't* Emilio, and this ceremony wouldn't bind them in the eyes of the law or God or *anyone*. They were going to do the legally binding ceremony later this afternoon, in Las Vegas. And in Vegas no one was going to *give* her to anyone. She was going to meet Johnny Anziano as an equal, as a business partner, and together they would stand before a justice of the peace and set in motion a business deal.

"*This* is the guy you manage to *scrounge* up only three days before your wedding?" Moira asked, opening the door again and peering out at Johnny again. "I think I'm going to steal your wedding gown, lock you in the closet, and marry him myself."

"He's doing it for the money," Chelsea told her, unable to resist taking a peek. But Moira shut the door before she could see him. "Is his tuxedo black?"

"Black and very nicely tailored. So tell me again where you found this guy? At an evening out at Chippendale's?"

"I'm scared to death and you're making jokes. What if he contests the annulment? Or challenges the prenuptial agreement?"

"What if he doesn't and everything works out hunky-dory?" Moira pointed out. "You get your money, he gets whatever percentage you've offered him, your parents get to throw their party. Everyone's happy. And, hey, you can give your ex my phone number after it's all over."

After it's all over. This part of it, the wedding and the reception, would be over in just a few hours. By three o'clock, she and Johnny would be on their way to Logan Airport. By four, they'd be in the air, heading for Las Vegas.

Chelsea closed her eyes, willing herself not to think beyond three o'clock, trying not to think about getting married for real. First things first, and first she had to get past this hurdle. Standing up in front of nearly six hundred people made her knees feel weak, and standing up in front of them to pledge eternal devotion to a man she had no intention of spending a month let alone an eternity with made her mouth dry.

And then there was the possibility that something could go wrong. Out of the six hundred wedding guests, what if one of them knew and recognized Johnny Anziano?

She took a deep breath, telling herself that she couldn't think that way. Everything was out of her hands now. All she had to do was hold on to the roller-coaster car and wait for this crazy ride to end at three o'clock. Three o'clock was only a few hours away. She could endure damn near anything for a few hours.

Her father opened the door and Moira slipped out, giving Chelsea a smile and a thumbs-up.

Howard Spencer looked impeccable, as usual. His salt-and-pepper hair was combed straight back from his face, each strand securely in place. He smiled at her, with a definite misty quality to his eyes. "Chelsea-bean, are you ready for this?"

She nodded, feeling a pang of remorse at her deception. Her father thought she was marrying for good, until death do us part. Not until annulment do us part. Still, when he found out, he'd probably congratulate her on her shrewd ability to get her hands on the money she so desperately needed.

Her father pulled her into his arms in a clumsy embrace. They weren't a touchy-feely family, the Spencers. They were the types who kissed the air next to someone's cheek or briskly shook hands.

For a fraction of a second Chelsea let herself imagine what it would have been like to grow up with a father who was more like the dad on *The Cosby Show* than a walking financial predictions computer.

But that kind of thinking was a waste of time. Her father was who he was. And her childhood was long since over.

"They're waiting for us," he told her. "Your mother's been seated and Moira and Sierra have just gone down the aisle." He opened the door and held out his arm for her.

The organ stopped playing as she moved toward the back of the church, toward the edge of the red carpet that had been rolled down the ordinary wood floor of the aisle. As she stood at her father's side in the back of the church, the organist began the traditional wedding march.

Here comes the bride. All dressed in white. For some reason, Chelsea could hear Bugs Bunny's voice in her head, singing the childish words that had been put to the tune. It would have been funny if she hadn't been so damn scared.

Everyone stood, turned to face the back of the church, smiling at her. Didn't they know she could barely breathe?

She searched for and found Moira's familiar face. Her friend and maid of honor was standing with Sierra at the altar. Her red hair had defied her attempts to tame it, and tendrils and curls escaped her French braid. On anyone else it would have looked messy, but on Moira it looked romantic and windswept.

Moira smiled at her, then turned slightly to glance across the aisle.

That was when Chelsea saw him.

Johnny Anziano.

The butterflies in her stomach exploded, flying everywhere, several of them lodging securely in her throat.

He had been right—his tuxedo was black, and it fit like a glove.

He looked impossibly good. He looked like one of those models in magazine ads where you knew the photo had been touched up because no one could possibly look so good in real life. The black of the tuxedo accentuated his trim waist and narrow hips, yet at the same time seemed to show off the broadness of his chest and shoulders. His legs looked fantastically long, and as she watched he shifted his weight slightly and the powerful muscles in his thighs moved against the soft fabric of his pants.

*In today's performance of Chelsea Spencer's*

*wedding, the part of the groom will be played by Giovanni Anziano.* This was totally insane.

He was watching her, his handsome face serious, his dark eyes intense. Their gazes locked and the butterflies that were left in her stomach accelerated the steps to their frantic dance.

She was actually going to marry this man.

She searched his eyes, wondering what he was thinking, wondering—inanely—whether or not he liked her dress. And then she was there. At the end of the aisle.

Her father lifted her veil, kissed her gently on the cheek, then handed her over to the man he thought was Emilio. But it wasn't Emilio, it was Johnny.

Johnny's hands were warm while hers were blocks of ice. He gave her a thoroughly relaxed smile. "Hey." How could he look so calm and cool?

Her own lips and face felt brittle, but she tried to position them into something approximating a smile too. "Hey."

Underneath his heavy lids, his gaze was as sharp as ever. "You okay?"

Chelsea nodded, the sound of his husky voice

somehow soothing her. She'd wanted to call him again last night as she had lain awake, tossing and turning. She'd liked talking to him on the phone the night before. She'd liked lying in the darkness of her bedroom, snuggling under her blankets, the phone and his voice nestled close to her ear. She'd liked it too much—and that was why she *hadn't* called him again.

"You sure?" he asked, his voice low. "You look a little pale. You know, it's okay if we call a time-out here."

Her smile felt more genuine this time. "We're not in the middle of a basketball game," she whispered back to him.

"Yeah, well, it's your wedding, right? You want a time-out, you can have a time-out."

"I'm fine, really." She took a deep breath, willing herself to be fine. Head up, shoulders back, nose slightly in the air. She'd learned it as a child. Stand as if you're in control, hold your body as if nothing that happens will perturb you in the least, maintain a slight disinterest, a distance from the events happening around you. It worked, as it nearly always did. She glanced at Johnny, raising one eyebrow very slightly. "I'm fine," she said again, and she was.

"Good." He was still watching her, as if he weren't quite sure whether or not to believe her.

The ceremony passed in a blur. She refused to think about the words she was saying as she promised to love and honor this man through richer and poorer, sickness and health. Till death do us part. She tried to repeat the words as nonsense syllables.

Johnny, too, spoke the wedding vows softly, as if he didn't want God overhearing his untruths.

She tried not to look at him as he slipped the wedding ring onto her finger, and as she did the same for him.

And then the minister declared them husband and wife. "You may kiss the bride."

This was the part she'd been dreading. She didn't want to kiss Johnny Anziano. She didn't want to—because she'd dreamed about kissing him when she finally fell asleep last night. And she'd dreamed it the night before too. And even the night before *that*.

Chelsea had dreamed about kissing this man the night after he'd saved her purse from those kids. Shoot, she'd *daydreamed* it moments after meeting him. And she was afraid that when his lips touched hers, he somehow would know.

She had a plan. She would wait until the last split second, and when his mouth was just a fraction of an inch away from hers, she would turn her head away and he would kiss her cheek.

In theory, it was a fine plan. In practice, it was thoroughly flawed.

Because he took his sweet time. He reached up and gently touched her face, pulling her chin and her mouth up to his, holding her firmly in place. That, combined with the warmth she could see as she looked into his eyes, was something her plan hadn't made provisions for.

And in a shot, all of her carefully maintained calm disintegrated, leaving her defenseless.

She couldn't pull away. The truth was, she didn't want to.

His lips brushed against hers in the gentlest, most chaste of kisses, and she felt a flash of disappointment. That was hardly a kiss.

But he wasn't done.

He kissed her again, still gently, but leaving no doubt in her mind as to what he wanted. He wanted a real kiss, a deep kiss, a curl-your-toes and melt-your-bones kind of kiss.

And she wanted it, too, God help her.

With a soft moan of disbelief, she parted her lips, meeting his tongue with her own. He tasted like sugar-sweetened coffee and peppermint, a combination that hardly seemed compatible.

It was sinfully delicious.

His mouth was warm and soft, his dizzying kiss so far beyond her fantasies, Chelsea almost laughed out loud.

But then she remembered. She was standing in a church filled with her parents' closest business associates and friends. She pulled back, and he released her. He was as shocked as she was—she could see it in his eyes.

The wedding guests were standing, applauding for them. Little did any of the six hundred realize, but they were cheering for Chelsea and John's first kiss. It was downright bizarre. Except as far as first kisses went, this one was *way* off the scale and thoroughly deserving of a round of applause.

Chelsea could feel Johnny slip his hand around her waist as he drew her down the altar steps toward the aisle that led out of the church. His touch was possessive, proprietary, and far too confident. He would take off her clothes that same way, she realized. Without hesitation, and as if taking possession of what naturally belonged to him.

He'd probably gotten far with a large number of women by simply taking control like that. Before they knew it, they were thoroughly seduced. And if that kiss at the altar was any indication, Chelsea had a sneaking suspicion that those women probably hadn't minded.

But she minded.

"The minister said you could kiss the bride— not inhale the bride," she whispered sharply as they plunged down the aisle.

There was amusement in Johnny's eyes. "Hey, it takes two, and I wasn't alone back there. You know that as well as I do."

He was right. She had kissed him as passionately as he'd kissed her. "I'm sorry," she said, at the exact moment he, too, apologized.

They were outside of the church, the heavy wooden doors separating them from the thundering organ music. They were alone—if only temporarily.

"No, *I'm* sorry," he said again. "You're right— I went too far. I knew you were off balance, and I took advantage of that. It's just...I've been dying to kiss you like that for a while now. I couldn't resist."

She made the mistake of gazing up into his eyes. Just a glimpse of the fire smoldering there was enough to make her heart pound.

"I still can't resist," he whispered, leaning forward to brush her lips with his.

He would have deepened the kiss again and she would have stood stupidly still and let him, were it not for the wedding photographer, who was striding toward them.

"*Perfect* picture," he enthused. "The absolutely *sweetest*, most genuine kiss I've ever taken. You're going to want that shot for your memory album, I can guarantee it. How about we get a few in front of the forsythia now?"

The look in Johnny's eyes was unmistakable. Underneath the rueful, good-natured humor was a clear message. He wanted more. And soon.

Dear God, Chelsea was in *big* trouble here.

Because she did too.

# SIX

"ABSOLUTELY NO TALK of business today," Johnny said for the twenty-seventh time. He spoke in what he considered his best "godfather" accent, but what Chelsea insisted sounded like Ricardo Montalban. What was wrong with these people, anyway? They seemed so surprised that he refused to talk business on his wedding day. If he were a doctor, would they be approaching him for free medical advice?

He could see Chelsea's blond head all the way across the elegant country-club ballroom and he excused himself and worked his way toward her.

She was talking with a group of elderly ladies. They were her great-aunts—at least that's the way he seemed to remember her introducing them on the receiving line. Some receiving line—everyone was so solemn and reserved.

In his neighborhood, people at a wedding smiled and laughed and kissed one another on the face or the mouth, and men embraced with resounding slaps on one another's backs. And the bride and groom started the dancing as soon as they arrived at the party. It was expected that they wouldn't stay long. They would barely even touch their dinners, instead escaping out the back door to celebrate their wedding in a far more private, intimate way.

He skirted the dance floor as he headed toward Chelsea. She'd been avoiding him rather skillfully since he'd kissed her outside of the church. That was going to stop. Right now.

He touched her arm and she glanced up at him, giving him a smile that didn't quite reach her eyes. She looked around for the quickest route to escape, but there was none. So she did the next best thing. She transformed into the Ice Princess.

This time he was ready. This time he was watching for it to happen, and sure enough, right before his very eyes, she turned into the Queen of Cool.

He bowed slightly to the older ladies. "You'll allow me the pleasure of dancing with my bride," he said to them.

Chelsea was the only one who protested as he gently pulled her onto the dance floor. "John, it's not time yet. We're not supposed to dance until—"

"Ladies and gentlemen," the bandleader said into his microphone. "May I present Emilio Giovanni and Chelsea Santangelo-Anziano-Spencer."

"What did he just say?" Even the Ice Princess couldn't keep from laughing, and when she did, Johnny caught a glimpse of the real Chelsea underneath.

"I told him we were hyphenating our names, and while I was at it, I thought I might as well throw in mine too. Santangelo-Anziano-Spencer. It has a nice ring to it, doesn't it?" He smiled. "Of course, our children will have to spend years in therapy to recover from having a name that doesn't fit on an address label."

She bristled. "There aren't going to be any children."

"Relax. I was making a joke." He pulled her into his arms as the band began to play.

But she pulled back slightly to gaze up at him. "This isn't the song I asked them to play."

"No, it's the song *I* asked them to play. The bandleader agreed it was more dignified than 'I'm Too Sexy for My Shirt.' "

"I recognize the melody, but I don't know the name," Chelsea said, frowning slightly.

Across the room, someone started tapping their water glass with their spoon—a request for the bride and groom to kiss.

"It's called 'Misty,' " he told her as a dozen more spoons joined in. "It's a jazz standard. You're probably not into jazz, right?"

She shook her head. "I listen to Top 40—when I have time to listen to the radio."

The ringing sound was unmistakable. He gazed into her eyes and caught a glimpse of trepidation— she knew what it meant. "They're not going to stop until I kiss you," he said softly.

She moistened her lips. "I know."

He lowered his head, but she stopped him, her voice low and serious.

"John, it's acting—you know that, right?"

"Acting."

"When we kiss each other," she explained. "When I kiss you...it's not real."

For a minute he just stared at her. She looked incredible. Her wedding dress was out of this world, with a snugly fitting top and a heart-stoppingly low-cut neckline. It was a dress that had been made to be worn with a Wonderbra, and Johnny was willing to bet that Chelsea had one on. His view, as he looked down at her, was something to behold. God bless the designer who had introduced that fashion phenomenon.

But despite his enticing view, it was Chelsea's eyes that kept drawing his gaze. She was looking at him calmly, steadily. Despite that one flash of nervousness he'd seen back at the church, she now seemed utterly cool and almost distant.

Johnny had always considered himself to be a good judge of women, in tune with their desires, aware of their needs. But Chelsea Spencer was a bundle of contradictions—one minute warm and friendly, filled with good humor and laughter, and the next cool and aloof, impossibly calculating and businesslike.

Which was the act?

Johnny had thought the Ice Princess was the disguise, but now he honestly didn't know.

*It's not real.*

The sound of the clinking was nearly deafening now, so he lowered his mouth to hers, kissing her harder and deeper than he probably should have. But hey, it wasn't real, right? And the wedding guests deserved to get their money's worth.

He pulled her closer, molding her slender body tightly against his as he took possession of her mouth. It wasn't real as she trembled, as she drove her fingers into his hair, as she kissed him back with a passion that took his breath away.

There was no way, plastered against him the way that she was, she could have failed to notice his instant hard-on. That was all too real.

She pulled back, a faint blush tingeing her cheeks, her eyes wide as she gazed up at him.

It was then, in that fraction of a second before Chelsea conjured up her Ice Princess persona, that he saw it. Molten desire burning in her eyes.

She was lying. The way she responded to him was real. And if that were true, he had to believe the Ice Princess was the act. It had to be.

"You're one hell of an actor," he murmured into her ear.

She didn't say a word.

"I'm glad Chelsea's finally found someone."

Johnny turned to see one of Chelsea's brothers standing next to him. No eyeglasses. It was Troy.

He looked more like Chelsea than the other brother did. He was blond and slender with a more masculine but no less elegant face.

"So has my little sister told you all the nasty family gossip?" he asked. "All of our dark secrets?"

Johnny shrugged. "We haven't had time to talk about much of anything besides the wedding plans."

"Oh, good, that means I can fill you in."

"I'm not sure I want to be filled in—"

"Yes, you do. You're part of the family now. You deserve to get a look at the skeletons in the closets. See the guy over there, about fifty years old, dark suit, bald spot, heading toward the bar?"

There were a dozen men who fit that description, but Johnny nodded anyway.

"He's my father's second cousin, Philip Spencer.

Former CEO of a company called Tristock. He spent eight years in jail for vehicular manslaughter. DUI. Got offered another job with the company on the day he got out. After all, he'd only killed a young woman—he hadn't done something truly awful like embezzle corporate funds. Oh, and look. See the couple sitting all alone at the table in the corner of the room?"

Johnny followed Troy's gaze.

"That's my cousin George and his wife. We don't remember what her name is, because she grew up in the projects in the South End. We call her George's Wife, or That Gold Digger from the Projects Who Married George. After all, it's obvious that she married Georgie for his money—never mind the fact that he chose to teach school instead of work for my uncle, and never mind the fact that he spent most of his share of my grandfather's trust on a tiny little house in the suburbs. The rest of it he's spending lavishly on renovations on that house so that the Wife can bake bread or something ridiculously low-class. See, she never went to college, which, as we all know, is either a sign of total stupidity, sheer slothfulness, or pure evil."

Troy clearly didn't buy in to any of what he was

saying, but Johnny couldn't keep from commenting. "Your family really believes that?" God, what would they think of him?

Troy rolled his eyes. "You should hear my uncle Ron—George's father—go on and on and *on* about the Wife. Sometimes even right in front of her, the tactless bastard. She could be a prizewinning rocket scientist, and my family would still call her That Girl from the Projects." He smiled at Johnny. "Don't worry about it—Chelsea told me you come from royalty."

"That shouldn't matter."

"Yeah, but in *this* family, it does."

"Excuse me," Johnny said. "I should go find Chelsea—"

But Troy caught his arm. "She's right there—dancing with Benton Scott—he's an old Harvard friend of mine."

Sure enough, Chelsea was on the dance floor, in the crush of dancers. She was laughing at something her partner said.

"When Chelsea was in high school, she had the biggest crush on Bent. He went out with her a few times, but it wasn't serious—she was seven years younger than he was. Then Bent knocked up his law-firm partner's daughter, and like a good little law clerk on the fast track toward making partner himself someday, he married the girl. Chelsea cried for about six months."

Johnny looked more closely at the man Chelsea was dancing with. He looked like money. Everything about him, from his perfectly coiffed dark blond hair to his quietly expensive tailored suit and his Hollywood movie-star face, screamed dollar signs. His fingernails looked manicured. His shoes were freshly shined, presumably by one of the servants. His straight white teeth gleamed as he laughed with Chelsea.

It was hard to imagine Chelsea crying for six months over anyone—except possibly this man. Who was married, and had gotten married not for love, but for money.

Just as Chelsea was in the process of doing.

Johnny headed for the bar, in search of a drink. He was willing to bet that he wasn't just a stand-in for Emilio, but that he was a stand-in for this Bent guy as well.

The revelation made him feel all kinds of things he didn't want to feel. Disgust. Envy. Frustration. Jealousy.

He wanted to go onto the dance floor and cut in. But that was stupid. Chelsea might have pretended to marry him in a church just a few hours ago. She was intending to marry him for real at a wedding chapel in Las Vegas before the day ended.

But he had no right to feel jealous. He wouldn't—and would probably never be—anything more to her than a business partner.

There was a line at the wedding chapel.

Johnny was still wearing his tuxedo. When he found out that they'd be going to the wedding chapel straight from the airport, he'd refused to change into jeans and a T-shirt for the flight. But he'd been comfortable enough on the plane to put his head back and go straight to sleep during the flight to Nevada, even without changing his clothes.

Chelsea had changed, though. She'd put on a pair of wide-legged white pants with a white silk blouse. It was what she would have chosen to get married in—if she'd had a choice. In fact, this Las Vegas setup was entirely the way she would have planned. The ceremony was going to be short and sweet, and she and Johnny were going to walk toward the justice of the peace together, as equals. And—if she had her way—they would seal the deal with a handshake.

She'd had enough of Johnny Anziano's soul-shattering kisses earlier today.

She glanced at her watch, trying her best not to be nervous. Why should she be? She'd done this once today already. The second time should be a piece of cake.

"What time does our flight to St. Thomas leave?" he asked.

Of course, this time when they said "I do," it would be for real. She had to clear her throat before she could speak. "In two hours."

"We have plenty of time."

"Yeah."

Johnny was watching her, his dark eyes unreadable. "So what *is* your favorite color?"

"Red." She glanced at him. "Yours?"

"Blue."

Chelsea looked down at the forms they'd had to fill out to get a marriage license. "I didn't even know how old you were until I read this."

"I'm twenty-six."

"Yeah, I can do the math. I minored in math in college."

"Now, you see, I didn't know that. What was your major?"

"I did a double major—computer science and physics. And then I went on to get my business degree."

Johnny whistled through his teeth. "Well, *I'm* impressed. I had no idea I was marrying a scholar."

"How about you? What was your major?"

He shook his head, smiling slightly. "I didn't go to college. At least not exactly."

Chelsea was embarrassed. She shouldn't have assumed. Quickly she changed the subject. "Your birthday's in October."

"Yep. I'm a Libra." He looked over her shoulder at the forms she held in her hand. "You were born late in January—an Aquarian, huh?"

She lifted an eyebrow. "Are we compatible?"

"Librans are pretty much compatible with everybody," he said with a smile.

"What a relief."

"What's your favorite holiday?"

Chelsea had to think. "I don't know. Christmas, I guess."

"Mine's New Year's Eve. It's such a high-energy night—everyone's all jazzed up for the coming year, with high expectations. And hope. The hope on that night is off the scale." He paused as the woman who was acting as a sort of hostess came out into the waiting room and took the couple who had arrived directly in front of them into the chapel.

They were next.

Johnny looked back at Chelsea. "Who's your favorite dead president?"

She blinked. "What?"

"For most people it's a toss-up between Washington and Lincoln, with Kennedy running a close third, but I'm an FDR fan, myself."

"I don't think I have a favorite president—dead or alive."

"You must've had one when you were a kid."

"When I was a kid, it was Washington," she said. "Definitely. That whole story about the cherry tree. 'Father, I cannot tell a lie, I chopped down the cherry tree.' I always thought he was a lot like Mr. Spock on *Star Trek*. Vulcans can't tell a lie, either. It's supposedly physiologically impossible."

"Except Spock *could* lie because he was half-human," Johnny pointed out.

"Which says a lot for humanity, doesn't it?" Chelsea sighed, her smile fading.

"You feel bad, don't you," he guessed perceptively, "for fooling all those people at the church today."

"My dad was so..." Chelsea shook her head, smiling ruefully. "God, for the first time during the twenty-eight years I've been alive, I actually saw him with tears in his eyes. All I could think of was the way I was lying to him." She miserably blew out a short explosion of air. "And not only was *I* lying to everyone, but I've gone and dragged you into it too."

"At least now when you go to hell, I'll be there with you, so you'll have someone to talk to."

"That makes me feel *so* much better."

"It's not too late to back out," he said. "We can just walk out of here, spend the next twenty-four hours playing the five-dollar blackjack table at Circus Circus and drinking beer with whiskey chasers on the house."

Chelsea had to laugh. "Sounds tempting."

"Then when we've had too much to drink to

keep our balance at the blackjack table, we can get a room upstairs and sleep it off for another twenty-four hours straight."

Sleep. As in share a bed. Yeah, right, they would sleep.

Johnny smiled, as if he were following her thoughts.

"I don't think so," she said.

"After a couple of days you could run home to your parents, claiming that Emilio was heavily into bondage and discipline, and that you left him, because that's not quite your style."

"How do you know that B and D isn't my style?" she couldn't resist asking.

He laughed in surprise, but recovered quickly. "Even if it is, I'm betting that you wouldn't share that fact with your mom and dad."

"Oh, that's a bet you'd win."

"Spencer and Anziano."

Chelsea looked up to see the wedding-chapel hostess beckoning to them. "Oh, God," she said. "It's time." She turned to Johnny. "It's not too late for you to back out."

"For seventy-five K," he told her, "I'm not going anywhere. Unless we can add to that Circus Circus scenario and say that after we get a room upstairs, we get to take turns tying each other up."

He hadn't realized that the wedding hostess was standing right behind him. He turned to see her there, and realized she'd overheard him. She was trying her best not to look shocked.

Johnny gave her one of his best smiles. "It's a wedding-night tradition in Chelsea's family," he said conspiratorially.

"He's kidding," Chelsea said, but the woman didn't look convinced.

As she followed the woman into the chapel she turned to give Johnny a chilling look.

"Oh, good, the Ice Princess is back," he said with a grin. "I was hoping I'd get to marry both of you—it'll make married life *really* interesting."

Ice Princess? Marry both...? "What are you talking about?" she asked, but he just smiled. With his light banter and silly questions, he'd managed to make her feel thoroughly relaxed. She liked having him around, she realized. And then she remembered those kisses. She liked having him around too much.

Chelsea's pulse started to accelerate at the thought that within the next few minutes she was going to marry this man, and she tried not to think, not to feel, not to anticipate.

The hostess took the forms they'd filled out and the copies of their birth certificates from Chelsea. "One moment, please."

"No kissing this time," she told him under her breath. "We shake hands, do you understand?"

"No way. The man says you may kiss the bride, not you may high-five the bride."

"This is a business deal. We should shake—"

"Where I come from, people embrace and kiss when a deal is made."

She stopped short. "Where *do* you come from?"

"I was born in the North End, but while I was growing up, I lived about a block away from the Projects."

"The . . . Projects?" It was an impossibly tough part of town, filled with gang violence, drug abuse, struggling welfare mothers, and drive-by shootings. And Johnny had grown up there.

"Yeah. I won't tell your daddy if you don't."

"Oh, God, someone told you about George's wife, Cathy."

"So she does have a name. Troy filled me in. Her status as a Projects kid hasn't exactly won her any popularity awards with the Spencer clan. Or should that be Klan, spelled with a *K*?"

Chelsea briefly closed her eyes. "I'm so sorry. You have every right to be offended."

"You can make it up to me—by letting me kiss the bride."

"John..."

He took her hand, squeezing her fingers gently. "Chelsea, this may be the only time I ever get married. Yeah, I'm doing it for the money, and yeah, it's weird, but please, let me at least do it right. And doing it right means when the guy says kiss the bride, I kiss the bride."

She gazed up at him. "It matters to you that much?"

"Yeah. It does. Absolutely."

"One kiss, and then you'll retire your lips—permanently?"

"Are you sure you want me to?" He lowered his voice. "I can do an awful lot with my lips—without running the risk of consummating this marriage."

Chelsea felt her cheeks heat. "I can't believe you just said that to me."

To her surprise, he actually looked embarrassed too. "I can't believe I did either." He took a deep breath. "Although, one thing my mother always taught me was, you can't have what you don't ask for."

"Please don't ask for more than I can give you," she said softly. "John, we talked about this when we signed the prenups. No sex. Of any kind. Just this one last kiss and that's it, all right?"

Johnny nodded. "If that's the way you want it..."

It wasn't the way she wanted it. It was the way she *needed* it to be.

"Giovanni Anziano and Chelsea Spencer?" The justice of the peace was a little, wizened old man wearing a western-cut jacket and an enormous cowboy hat. "Please approach."

"I don't know about you," Johnny whispered almost silently to her as they moved forward, "but the hat works for me."

"Chelsea Jasmine Spencer, do you take Giovanni Vincente Anziano as your lawfully wedded husband?"

Chelsea took a deep breath. "I do."

"And do you, Giovanni Vincente Anziano take Chelsea Jasmine Spencer—"

"I do."

The justice of the peace gazed at Johnny from the narrow band between the top of his half glasses and the wide brim of his hat. "In a hurry there, are you, son?"

"Yes, sir."

He smacked the counter with a gavel. "By the power vested in me by the state of Nevada, I pronounce you man and wife."

Johnny looked at Chelsea in surprise. "That's it?"

"I asked for the short version. I hope you don't mind."

He looked at the judge. "We're married?"

"You truly are. Go ahead, son," the old man said. "Kiss your bride."

Chelsea braced herself, but Johnny didn't move. He just gazed at her.

"This time's for real," he told her.

Chelsea nodded. Yes. This time it was real. This time they were really married.

He moved closer then, drawing her into his arms before he lowered his mouth and then...

He kissed her.

This time, it was real. This time, he wrapped her in his arms as if he intended never to let her go.

This time, his lips were impossibly gentle, his mouth impossibly sweet.

And this time, when her heart pounded crazily, she had no excuses handy.

Still, she let herself kiss him, losing herself in the sweetness of their embrace. Because he was right. Because this could very well be the only time she ever got married too. Because he was quite possibly the most desirable man she'd ever met. Because despite that, from this moment forth, their relationship was going to be pure business.

She was going to make damn sure of that.

# SEVEN

"You bought me a *present*?"

Johnny smiled at Chelsea's look of total amazement as she turned to gaze at the neatly wrapped and beribboned package he had put into her hands.

They were sitting in the first-class section of a jet heading directly to the Caribbean. He was on his way to paradise with the most beautiful, most appealingly complex and attractive woman he'd ever had the pleasure to meet. But just a short time ago she'd given him his final warning. This wasn't a honeymoon. It was a four-day-three-night-long business meeting.

In other words, hands off.

He'd never seduced a woman with his hands tied behind his back before. But there was a first time for everything.

Oh, not that he'd go and mess up her chances for getting an easy annulment. No, he could wait. But by the day that the annulment was declared, he was determined that Chelsea Spencer would be more than ready to fall into bed with him. And then they would consummate and celebrate their *not* being married to their hearts' content.

"What are *you* smiling at?" she asked, but he just shook his head, watching as she unwrapped the gift he'd bought for her. She opened the little cardboard box. "It's a . . . What *is* it?"

"It's a miniature music box." He fingered the unfamiliar weight and bulk of the thick gold wedding ring on his left hand. "If you wind the little key on the bottom, it'll play a very square version of 'Harlem Nocturne.' "

Intrigued, she wound the key and laughed as the melody came tinkling out. "I know this song."

"It's supposed to swing a whole lot more, but there's not much you can do with an old-fashioned cylinder-style music box that's this small. I'm amazed they managed to fit eight bars of the tune onto something that tiny."

"It's such a pretty melody." She looked up at him almost shyly. "This is so sweet."

"I'm glad you like it." Damn, it would be so easy to lose himself in her blue eyes. . . .

"I feel like a jerk—I didn't get you anything."

"In that case, I'll let you pick up the tab on the champagne."

"Champagne?"

Chelsea watched as Johnny gestured for the flight attendant. The young woman came over almost immediately, ready with a big smile and a flutter of her eyelashes. "Yes, sir?"

Johnny reached for Chelsea's hand, turning it over to look at her wristwatch. "In about three minutes we'll be celebrating our two-and-a-half-hour wedding anniversary. Do you think you can get a bottle of champagne opened in time?"

"Only two and half hours since you were married? Oh, aren't you so sweet!" She rushed toward the food-preparation area.

"Two and a half hours," Chelsea echoed. Johnny was still holding her hand, and she gently pulled it free. "Are you sure you don't want to skip the fractions and go for the solid hours—wait for three to celebrate?"

"I'm not real good at waiting." He fished in his jacket pocket, trying to pull something free. "Besides, we need to have something to drink right now—to wash down our wedding cake."

He tossed a double package of Twinkies onto the tray table.

Chelsea looked from Johnny to the Twinkies and back. "*That's* your idea of wedding cake?" She couldn't keep from laughing.

"I could have done a whole lot better if I'd had a couple hours and a bakery kitchen," he admitted. "Instead, all I had to work with was an airport vending machine. It was this or Yodels. And I figured wedding cakes are supposed to be vanilla, so..."

Chelsea picked up the Twinkie package. "There's no way in hell you're going to get me to eat one of these."

"You don't have to eat an entire Twinkie," he told her, somehow managing to keep a perfectly straight face. "You just need to take a little, tiny bite."

"I eat only healthy food," she told him, still

laughing. "Twinkies are the total antithesis of both healthy *and* food. No way is this getting anywhere near *my* mouth."

"But isn't eating the wedding cake supposed to bring good luck?" Johnny asked, tearing the package open. "Don't we risk the wrath of the wedding-cake god if we don't partake? Isn't that, like, bad juju or something?"

"Believe me, it would be *very* bad juju for me to take even the tiniest bite of one of these."

He took a bite and waved the half-eaten Twinkie in front of her nose. "Sure I can't tempt you with its flavorful aroma?"

She laughed, pushing his hand away. "Oh, God, it smells like my elementary-school cafeteria. Tiffany Stewart *always* brought three packs of Twinkies in her lunch—she told her housekeeper that there was a special table where privileged students could leave food donations for the scholarship kids, and since her father had more money than God, her housekeeper always let her take two extra packs. Of course, there was no such table. Tiffany threw away her sandwich and existed on a pure Twinkie diet for about three years."

"You went to a private school, huh?" he asked.

"The Wellford Academy. Pre-K through twelfth grade."

The flight attendant brought two plastic glasses of champagne. "Congratulations." She turned to Chelsea, nearly beaming with happiness. "You're so lucky—he's good-looking *and* romantic."

"So why is it you're not married?" Chelsea asked, taking a sip of her champagne after the attendant had walked away.

He gazed at the cabin lights through the plastic glass and the bubbling wine. "Just unlucky, I guess."

She shifted in her seat to face him. "I sense a story here."

He took a sip of his champagne. "I thought you didn't want to get to know me that well."

He was right. She shouldn't be asking him questions. She shouldn't try to find out who he was, where he'd been, what he thought, how he felt. She should keep her distance. She turned away, forcing herself to feel nothing but detached. It was only a matter of time before she received her inheritance and this whole ridiculous game ended. All she had to do was endure. She could do that. She *would* do that. "You're right. I don't. Consider the question withdrawn."

She signaled for the flight attendant, who appeared almost instantly. "I'd like a pillow and blanket, please."

Johnny cursed softly. The sudden chilly drop in the cabin's temperature was his fault. He'd gone and conjured up the Ice Princess—because of the one subject he didn't want to discuss.

"Thank you," Chelsea said politely to the attendant, who had handed her a pillow and blanket. "You can take the champagne, too, please. I'm done."

"She was from Paris." Johnny waited for the attendant to leave before he spoke. "Her name was Raquel, and I was with her for three years—"

Chelsea reclined her seat. "I really don't want to hear this."

"We were pretty hot and heavy right from the start, and the last two years we actually lived together. This was down in Washington, D.C.—we were both students at the International Culinary Institute. Can you imagine someone coming to America from Paris to learn how to cook? I would have sold my soul for a chance to study in Paris."

He'd gotten her attention. "You know how to cook?"

"Some people think so. Anyway, Raquel's dad had a heart attack, and she had to fly home. She was supposed to be gone for a month, but she never came back. She wrote me a letter telling me to toss her stuff. She said she didn't need it. And oh, by the way, by the time I got the letter, she would already be married to some old family friend. Two *years* we lived together, and she types me a note."

"I'm sorry," she said quietly.

"Yeah, I was too. But before that I was angry, and then I was hurt. I thought you know, first you live together and then you get married. It seemed the natural order of events—not first you live together and then you marry someone else. I had no clue she didn't feel the same way I did. I mean, right up until she left—the night before her flight home we..." He shook his head, smiling ruefully. "No, you definitely don't want to hear about that. Sorry."

They sat for a moment in silence.

"I guess I got you on the rebound, so to speak," Chelsea finally said.

"It's been five years. I think I'm past the rebound stage."

"But you still haven't found somebody new."

"Nope. But then again, I haven't exactly been looking. I work kind of crazy hours. Don't get me wrong—I haven't exactly been a monk these past five years. I've had girlfriends—I just haven't let anything get too serious."

Chelsea was watching him. The Ice Princess had vanished. There was nothing but compassion and warmth in her eyes.

"Do you still love her?" she asked quietly.

"No," he said. But he could tell from the way she was watching him that she didn't believe him.

"How about you?" he asked. "Do you still love what's-his-name? Bent?"

Her eyes widened. "Who told you about Bent?"

"Troy."

"Troy *knows*?"

"Knows what? Troy told me you had some kind of teenage crush on his friend—that you guys dated a few times and then he married some girl he got pregnant."

Chelsea was curled up in her seat, her cheek pressed against the reclined back, watching him, as if deciding how much to tell him. She hitched her blanket up higher underneath her chin. "Troy didn't know, but Bent and I did more than date," she finally said. "It was really just dumb luck that he didn't manage to get me pregnant too."

"How old were you?"

She paused before answering, her eyes assessing him, trying to gauge his reaction. "Sixteen."

In his neighborhood, girls lost their virginity at age sixteen all the time. But in hers? He did his best to hide his shock. "And he was how many years older?"

"He was twenty-three."

"Christ, what the hell was he thinking?" So much for hiding his shock.

Chelsea smiled. "I don't think Bent particularly paid attention to the parts of his anatomy that did the thinking. And as for me, I was impetuous and independent, and trying much too hard to be all grown-up." She laughed, rolling her eyes. "I was so naive. When he told me that Nicole was pregnant—that was her name, Nicole—I honestly didn't understand. I thought he was somehow being coerced into marrying some dumb girl who'd gotten herself into trouble. It took me two days before I made the connection that he'd been sleeping with Nicole on the nights he wasn't with me. It was a crash course in reality."

"You were just a kid—it must've been hell to have to deal with that."

"I didn't deal with it very gracefully," she admitted. "It took me years to get over the bastard. You know, the really stupid thing was, if he had been faithful, if he had really honestly loved me, I would have married him right out of college. I would've become everything that I hated most about my mother and my sister, and all those other good little wives who live and breathe only for their husbands. I would have been driven slowly insane. Nicole saved me years of expensive therapy, attempting to discover the underlying causes of my deep unhappiness."

"How do you know you would have been unhappy?"

"Oh, *please*."

"No, I'm serious." Johnny reclined his own seat, so that they were nearly nose to nose. "I met your sister, Sierra. She seems really happy. And her husband, Ed Pope—he seems like an okay guy. True, he's not *your* type, *you* wouldn't be happy with him, but maybe your sister is. Not everybody wants to be president of their own company, you know." He gazed at her, well aware that she hadn't answered his question. She hadn't told him whether or not she was still in love with her former—and probably her first—lover.

"But *I* want to be president of my own incredibly successful business," she told him. "How could I do that with a husband like Edgar Pope or Benton Scott, who at any moment could come home and tell me he's being transferred to the Philadelphia office?"

"Obviously the trick is to marry someone like me. A townie. Even if Lumière's burned down, I'd find another job in Boston. It's my home—I'm not going anywhere, except on vacation."

"Except—suppose that we were really married, suppose we really were trying to make it work," she said. "And what if I had the opportunity to sell my business for a million dollars to a buyer in Texas—with the contingency that I move to Dallas and continue on in my salaried position as president for the next five years?"

"Five *years*?"

"You wouldn't want to do it."

Johnny shook his head. "There's no way I can know what I would or wouldn't do. I mean, everything would be different. If we loved each other..." He shrugged. "If I loved you and you were in Dallas... Hell, I guess I'd go to Dallas. If I knew I could go back to Boston in five years—"

"What if you didn't know that?" she asked. "What if you didn't know where you'd end up, whether you'd stay in Dallas *another* five years, or then go somewhere totally different? And what if the only job you could get was at a Texas barbecue restaurant, waiting tables? And what if you knew that the ten most talented chefs from Paris were coming to Boston to spend a year teaching a small group of students—and you'd been chosen to participate?"

Johnny had to laugh. "Well, that would make the choice a little tougher. I'd see if we could compromise—you'd put off selling the business for a year and after that I'd go to Dallas."

"What if the deal wouldn't wait a year? What if it had to happen immediately?"

She was damned good at thinking up worst-case scenarios. "God, Chelsea, I don't know."

"Or here's a good one: What if I didn't tell you

about the deal until after it had been done? What if you didn't have a choice? What if I just came home and said, 'Guess what, honey? We're moving to Dallas!' "

Johnny was silent.

"Both my mother and Sierra have lived that scenario more than once," she told him. "But I refuse to put myself into that situation. Because if it were *you* who had to go to Dallas, and I was the one who had to give up my job and my home and my friends...I wouldn't go." She gazed at him unblinkingly. "And *that's* why I'll never get married."

"Hey. Hey, Chelsea. Seat-belt sign's on. We're coming in for a landing...."

Chelsea stirred. She was so comfortable and *so* soundly asleep, but now someone was touching her shoulder, trying to wake her up.

"Time to sit up," the voice said again. It was a familiar voice, husky and deep and sexy. She'd recognize that voice anywhere. It was...It was...?

"If you sit up, you can see the sunrise. It's incredible—you've got to get a look at this."

The voice was very persuasive—and very

familiar. Why couldn't she remember who it belonged to?

"Please let this just be a dream," Chelsea mumbled, snuggling into her pillow. "I'm too tired to wake up."

"Come on, sleepyhead, open your eyes."

"They're open," she murmured.

He laughed, and she remembered who he was. He was her husband.

Her *husband*...?

Chelsea opened her eyes and found herself staring directly at the fly on Johnny Anziano's pants. She sprang up, bumping her back on the tray table in front of her seat and hitting her head on the luggage compartment.

She had been sleeping with her head in his lap.

"Whoa," he said, reaching out to steady her and help her down into her seat.

"I'm sorry." She was out of breath, her heart pounding. "I didn't know I'd taken over your seat as well as mine."

"I didn't mind."

Chelsea found herself gazing into Johnny's chocolate-brown eyes. He was smiling very slightly and she knew he was telling the truth. He hadn't minded. In fact, on the contrary...

Her hair was falling down, and she used the excuse to look away from him as she pulled the remaining pins free. Searching her handbag, she found her brush and ran it through her hair.

"Check out the sunrise," he said, gesturing out the window.

It was amazing. The tops of the clouds were pink and orange and glowing. It didn't look real, yet there they were.

There they were, indeed.

He shifted uncomfortably in his seat.

"Did you sleep at all?" Chelsea had to ask.

Johnny didn't say yes or no. He just smiled. "I'm fine."

In fact, he was better than fine. True, he hadn't slept, but he hadn't wanted to sleep. Chelsea had fallen fast asleep, leaning against the side of the plane. But then she'd shifted, trying to get comfortable, resting her head against his shoulder. He'd pulled up the armrests that were between their two seats in an effort to make her even more comfortable, and his movement had pushed her down so that her head was on his lap.

That had fueled a few hundred thousand fantasies or so.

He'd allowed himself the luxury of touching her silky-smooth hair. It was baby fine and so soft underneath his fingers, glistening in the dim cabin light like the most precious gold.

He'd spent the night watching her gentle breathing, letting her hair slide between his fingers, thinking about all that she'd told him.

If Chelsea loved him, *really* loved him, there was no place he wouldn't go to be with her. Dallas, Boston, Timbuktu. If she were there, he'd be there, guaranteed. *If* she loved him.

But she'd made it more than clear that love wasn't on her agenda.

He'd spent some time thinking about Benton Scott. Chelsea had been in love with the man—maybe she was still in love with him. If there were ever a guy more different from Johnny than night was from day, it was Benton Scott.

Could the man's name sound any more Anglo-Saxon? He was one of Troy's *Harvard* chums. He was the crown prince of the "us" club, while Johnny was the heir apparent of "them," born into his place—or lack of place—in the social registry, the same way Bent Scott had been born into his.

Money. Education. Bent Scott had it over Johnny in every way imaginable. Looks. A woman who went for fair-haired, blue-eyed, slender men like Bent wouldn't give Johnny a second glance.

Night and day.

He'd had to stop and untangle a lock of Chelsea's hair from where it had gotten caught around his wedding band, and he'd realized something he'd been trying his best to ignore.

It wouldn't take much for this woman to entangle herself around his heart. If he wasn't careful, he could very easily fall head over heels in love... with his wife.

# EIGHT

"YOU SURE I can't talk you into coming into the water?" Johnny asked. "It's *great*. You should see the fish, just swimming around out there—all colors, like something you'd see in someone's tank, only *huge*. They'll swim right up to you."

Chelsea looked up from her powerbook to see Johnny smiling at her, water dripping off of his hard-muscled body, his wet hair plastered against his head, water beading on his eyelashes.

His bathing suit was the loose-fitting, knee-length kind, but on him, it looked transcendently sexy.

Standing there on the white sand, with the turquoise Caribbean ocean and the crystal-blue Caribbean sky behind him, her husband looked like a walking, breathing advertisement for hedonistic temptations.

Husband in name only, she reminded herself.

He held out his hand. "Come on, Chelsea. You can do whatever you're doing later, can't you?"

She steeled herself before looking into his eyes. "I really can't," she lied. "I have to fax these reports to Moira first thing in the morning."

He sat down on the edge of the lounge chair next to hers. "Okay," he said reasonably. "You take a couple of hours, finish up those reports, and then we'll have dinner together. I was reading one of the guidebooks about this place called the Mafali—it's an open-air restaurant up on the side of the mountain, overlooking the harbor. The food's not fancy—mostly grilled steaks, but the view's supposed to be—"

"I can't."

"—fabulous. Why not?"

He knew damn well why not. Sure, she could give him more excuses. She had more reports to write, more work to do. She'd brought enough with her to keep her occupied every waking moment of this trip. But she didn't want to play games.

"I don't want to have dinner with you," she told him bluntly. "I don't want to pretend that we're newlyweds, I don't even want to be friends with you. I think it would be best if we just went our separate ways over the next three days."

Johnny laughed. "This is perfect," he said, shaking his head in disbelief. "Here I've gone and *married* you, and you *still* won't go out on a date with me. How pathetic is that?"

It was pathetic. But she couldn't help it. She couldn't dare let herself get any closer to him. Instead of waking up with her head in his lap, God knows where she'd find herself waking up next.

"I can't talk you into changing your mind?"

Chelsea shook her head. She refused to acknowledge the disappointment she could see in his eyes. She focused all of her attention on her powerbook screen as she tried to distance herself from him, to pull back, to not care. After all, disappointment was a part of life.

From the corner of her eye, she could see him, still sitting next to her, just watching her work for several long minutes after she had, in a sense, dismissed him.

Finally, he stood up and walked away.

Chelsea looked up then, unable to resist watching him head for the resort bar, unable truly to keep her distance, despite what she would have him believe.

Because she cared. Somehow Giovanni Anziano had gotten under her skin, and try as she might, she couldn't help but care.

"Do the names Edward and Susan Farber ring any bells?" Johnny said into the telephone as soon as Chelsea picked up.

"Um," she said, "yeah. The Farbers. Friends of my parents—from the country club, I think?" He could picture her doing a mental double take, realizing what he had asked her. Her voice went up an octave. "Oh my God, are they *here*?"

"They're sitting in the resort dining room right this very minute," he told her.

Chelsea swore sharply. "Have they seen you?"

"Of *course* they've seen me." Johnny let his frustration ring in his voice. This trip wasn't turning out the way he'd hoped—not by a long shot. The last time he'd even gotten within range of Chelsea had been two days earlier, in the afternoon, on the beach. She'd been plugged into her computer and had barely even looked up to tell him to forget about dinner, forget about talking, forget about *any*thing. She wasn't interested. Since then, she'd done her best to avoid him. "You don't honestly expect that I'd recognized *them* after meeting them for fifteen seconds in a receiving line—two out of the five hundred and something people I met for the first time a few days ago?"

"You sound annoyed." There was real surprise in her voice.

"I *am* annoyed. You better get your butt down here, unless you want Eddie and Sue getting the word back to Mumsy and Dadsy that they saw Chelsea's bridegroom eating dinner all by himself three days after the wedding."

"Can't you come up—pretend we're ordering in tonight?"

"No," Johnny told her flatly. "I was already sitting in the restaurant when they saw me. I told them you were running late—that you'd be down in a minute."

There was silence on the other end of the phone. "You're mad at me, aren't you?" she finally asked.

He had to answer her truthfully. "No," he said. "Not mad. Disappointed. I thought we were starting to become friends."

He heard her sigh, heard the rustling of papers on the other end of the telephone. "Have you ordered your dinner yet?"

"Yes, I did. I thought I'd give the so-called chef a chance to ruin some swordfish steaks tonight."

She laughed nervously. "Wow, this is a side of you I've never seen before."

"Yeah, well, I guess the honeymoon's over, huh?"

"Could you order me a large salad?" she asked. "No cheese, no bacon, vinaigrette dressing on the side? Then give me three minutes, and I'll be right down."

Johnny hung up the phone and briefly closed his eyes. God bless the Farbers. Chelsea was going to have dinner with him.

It took Chelsea a little bit longer than three minutes, but not much. When Johnny spotted her coming into the lobby, she was wearing a loose-fitting, long flowing blue island print sundress, and her hair was up on top of her head.

She looked beautiful, and Johnny let himself stare while she was still all the way across the room, while she stopped at the Farbers' table and said a brief hello. He knew that once she sat down across from him, he wouldn't be able to look at her this way. She wouldn't want him to.

How the hell had he ever gotten himself into this situation?

"Hi," she said almost shyly, and he rose to his feet to greet her.

"How's work?" he asked, sitting down across from her.

There was a candle in the middle of the table, and its flickering flame threw light and shadows across Chelsea's face as she gazed at him. "I've gotten quite a bit done." She looked out across the patio, toward the beach and the moonlit water. "It's a beautiful evening, isn't it?"

Johnny felt a flash of frustration. Small talk. They could go on like this all night. But he didn't want to talk about the weather. He had bigger fish to fry. He leaned forward. "I don't understand what the problem is, Chelsea," he told her. "I signed the agreements you wanted me to sign, and I promised to keep sex out of the picture. I gave you my word, but you won't trust me. And I'm finding that hard to deal with."

He more than expected her to slip into Ice Princess mode and regard him with haughty disdain. But she didn't. Instead, she sighed, and gazed out at the moonlight, unable to meet his eyes. Up close like this, she looked a little anxious and a little tired, as if she weren't sleeping well at all. "I guess you don't want to talk about the weather."

"The weather here is perfect. There's nothing to say about it."

Chelsea took a sip from her water glass, trying to pretend that her hand wasn't shaking as she glanced up at him. "So what *do* you want to talk about? My deeply rooted problem with trust? It probably goes back to my childhood—we could be here for quite some time."

"I've got time."

Chelsea let herself really look at the man sitting across the table from her. He was quite possibly the man they had in mind when they coined the phrase *tall, dark, and handsome*. He usually seemed to be on the verge of smiling—except for now. Right now he was uncharacteristically solemn, his dark eyes sober yet no less intense as he watched her.

"Maybe we could start by talking about something easier," Chelsea said.

"You're afraid of me, because I'm legally your husband," he guessed with unerring perception.

She drew in a deep breath. "Or we could start with something even harder."

"Or maybe you're afraid that you're going to like being married to me too much."

Chelsea forced a laugh. "Don't be ridiculous—"

"Why don't you tell me what the problem is, then?" He spoke softly, urgently. He really wanted to know. "We were doing fine on the flight from Vegas, then all of a sudden, we're at the hotel and you're telling me that you don't even want to be my *friend*? What the hell is that about? What did I do? Did I offend you in some way? Chelsea, did I say or do something that makes you think you can't trust me?"

She briefly closed her eyes, then told him the truth. It was the least she could do. "I do trust you," she said, gazing at him in the candlelight. "It's my own self I don't have any faith in."

Johnny struggled to understand. He couldn't believe what he had just heard. "You don't trust *yourself...*?"

"To stay away from you," she finished softly, glancing up at him almost shyly, her eyes filled with chagrin.

He was stunned. Of all the things he'd expected her to say, that was last on the list.

"Every time I'm near you, I want...things I shouldn't want," she admitted quietly. "I can't stop thinking about the way you kissed me...."

She looked away from him, as if embarrassed, and Johnny reached for her hand, moving out of his own chair and into the seat next to hers, wanting to reassure her she was not alone. "Is that really so awful?" he asked.

"Yes." She spoke vehemently, her blue eyes sparking as she looked up at him, but still, she didn't pull her hand away.

He tried to make a joke. "Last time I checked, no one went to hell for kissing."

"It's not the kissing—it's where those kisses would lead that has me worried."

Where those kisses would lead...They wouldn't lead anywhere—at least not if he kissed her here, in the resort's restaurant. And not if he kissed her anyplace else, either. Not unless both of them absolutely wanted it to.

Johnny leaned even closer to her, catching her chin with his other hand. Her skin was as soft and as smooth as he remembered, and he felt a wave of giddiness. He was going to kiss her. Right now. The way he'd been dying to kiss her since Vegas. "Let's try it and see exactly where it will lead."

"John—" She tried to pull away and he let her go.

But his soft words kept her from standing up and running away. "The Farbers are watching."

Johnny saw her glance across the room, saw all of her uncertainty and trepidation in her eyes. But he saw longing too. And he knew without a doubt that she wanted him to kiss her—as much, if not more, than she *didn't* want him to kiss her.

He leaned forward, closing the gap between them, capturing her mouth with his, drinking her in. Whether she parted her lips willingly or in surprise, he didn't know—and he didn't care. For every inch she gave him, he was determined to take a mile. He pulled her closer, touching the softness of her arms and the delicate fabric of the dress that covered her back. He kissed her harder, deeper, feeling her hands against the back of his neck, first tentatively, then possessively, as she kissed him with equal abandon.

And he knew in that instant that he was dead wrong. This kiss wasn't just a kiss. It didn't lead nowhere. In fact, it did quite the opposite. It led directly to temptation. It burned an unswerving path out of the restaurant, into the lobby, and up the stairs to the second floor, where they had adjoining suites. It pushed open the door to Chelsea's bedroom and flung them both down upon her bed, arms and legs intertwined, clothing quickly removed until they were pressed together, skin to skin, soft flesh against hard muscle, straining to become one.

The images that flashed into his mind were sharp and clear. Chelsea, naked, on her bed. Pale skin, perfect and smooth. Blond hair like spun gold fanned out against the stark white of the sheets. Her smile of welcome as she reached for him. Her soft hands gliding across his body. Her drawn-in breath and the expression of sheer pleasure on her face as he filled her ...

With herculean effort, Johnny pulled back,

away from Chelsea's lips. He watched her eyes flutter open, watched her pulse pounding in her delicate throat.

His own breathing was ragged, and as she met his eyes he knew he'd only succeeded in thoroughly proving himself wrong.

"Okay," he said, reaching for alternatives. "So we *don't* kiss. We can spend tomorrow together and just...not kiss."

She put her head in her hands. "How did I ever get myself into this?"

"Tomorrow's our last day here. I just want to be with you, Chelsea. I want to *talk* to you—"

She didn't even lift her head. "I don't think I'm strong enough."

"I can be strong enough for both of us."

"But if you can't?"

"I can," he insisted. "This is about more than just sex. I want to go to the beach with you tomorrow. I want to show you this great place to snorkel—I want to spend the day with you."

She rested her chin in her hand, looking at him for several long seconds before she spoke, searching his eyes, as if trying to read his mind. "And what about tonight?"

Johnny took a deep breath. "I can say good night to you at the door to your room and then walk away. I can do that."

Her eyes lingered on his lips and she didn't try to hide her attraction for him as she looked back up into his eyes. "And what if I tell you I want you to kiss me again? What if I ask you to come into my room and spend the night with me? Would you be strong enough to turn me down?"

"I don't know—" He cut himself off as he held her gaze, as he, too, let her see how badly he wanted her. "No," he said honestly. "No, I wouldn't be."

Time seemed to stretch way out as they looked into each other's eyes, the truth laid out on the table before them.

Chelsea was the first to look away. She took a sip of her water, knowing that it wouldn't help at all to cool her down. "Tomorrow, if you see the Farbers at the beach," she said, amazed that her voice could sound so normal, "tell them I've had too much sun—that's why I'm not with you."

Johnny nodded. "Yeah, all right."

The waiter appeared, carrying Chelsea's salad and his swordfish steak.

Johnny looked up at him. "Sorry for the inconvenience," he said, "but can you have room service bring this up to our rooms?"

"No problem at all, sir." The food disappeared back toward the kitchen.

Johnny got to his feet, holding out his hand for Chelsea. "Come on," he said. "Let's make it look good for the Farbers."

Chelsea stood and he pulled her close, looping his arm around her shoulders. She caught a glimpse of Susan Farber's knowing smile as they left the restaurant.

If Susan Farber only knew...

Chelsea was stepping into the warm water of a bath when the phone rang. Thinking it could only be Moira, she sat down among the bubbles and reached for the telephone's bathroom extension.

"It's about time that you called," she said as a greeting as she nestled the phone against her ear.

There was a pause, then a voice that was decidedly *not* Moira's spoke. "I don't know who exactly you expect this to be, but it's not. It's me."

It was Johnny Anziano. Chelsea nearly dropped

the receiver into the bubbly water. She was un-
dressed and in the bathtub, which seemed an utterly inappropriate place to have a conversation
with him.

"I thought you were Moira," she admitted.

"Well, I'm not," he said.

She stood up, water sheeting off of her as she
reached for her towel. But she stopped mid-grab,
catching sight of her reflection in the big mirror
over the double set of sinks. She was naked, her
body glistening in the dim light of the candle she'd
brought into the bathroom. But so what if she was
naked? Johnny couldn't see her. And if she got out
of the tub to talk to him, the water would be cold
by the time she got back in.

Besides, it would be fun to talk to him, knowing
that he'd damn near have a heart attack if he knew
where she was and what she was doing. She could
just imagine the look on his face....

She sat down among the bubbles, smiling at the
thought. "What's up?"

"You know, it just suddenly occurred to me that
we could talk on the phone." His voice was smoky
and resonant—and capable of sending shivers
down her spine and heat coursing through her

entire body. "You're over there and I'm over here, and the door's locked between us, so the whole temptation thing is pretty much taken care of."

He was right. They could talk on the phone without running the risk of winding up in each other's arms. And she wanted to talk to him. She *liked* talking to him. She leaned her head back and closed her eyes. "What do you want to talk about?"

He didn't hesitate. "You."

She opened her eyes. "That's not fair. How come we can't talk about *you*?"

"We can take turns," he suggested. "I'll ask you a question, and then you can ask me one."

"How come you get to go first?"

Johnny laughed. "All right. *You* go first."

"Okay." Chelsea gazed up at the moisture dripping down the steamy tile walls. It seemed to gleam in the candlelight. She sank down into the water until the bubbles covered all but the tops of her breasts. "Let's see.... What kind of car are you going to buy with the seventy-five grand?"

He laughed again. He had a really fabulous laugh. "Who says I'm going to buy a car?"

"The woman at Meals on Wheels told me you

drive an ancient VW Bug," Chelsea told him, sinking farther into the water, so that the back of her head was wet, careful not to drop the receiver in. "Allegedly, the car's already died, but both you and it refuse to acknowledge that."

"That car's a classic," Johnny told her. "I might spend a few hundred dollars getting a tune-up, but no way am I buying a new car."

She sat up, squeezing the water out of her hair with her free hand, then reached for the soap. "What kind of man would prefer a museum artifact to a zippy new sports car...?"

"The kind of man who's saving all of his money so he can open his own restaurant," Johnny told her.

"Is *that* what you're going to do with the money?"

"That's right."

She lathered up her washcloth. "What kind of restaurant?"

"The best," he said. "The kind where people drop huge bills for dinner, and leave feeling they got the better end of the deal because the food was so good."

"I had no idea," Chelsea murmured, tucking the

phone under her chin as she ran the washcloth up her arm.

"Are you . . . splashing?"

"Splashing?" Chelsea asked.

"Yeah," he said. "It sounds like you're splashing. Like, with water?"

The slightly rough texture of his voice seemed to slide exquisitely against her skin, like the sensation of the soapy washcloth against her breasts and stomach. "Really?"

"There it is again," Johnny said. "Holy God, you're in the tub, aren't you?" His voice sounded odd—choked and tight, as if he were suddenly having trouble breathing.

She smiled, lifting one leg to run her washcloth from her ankle to her thigh. "I take baths at night to relax."

She heard him draw in a deep breath, and when he spoke again, his voice was intimate and low. "So how's it going? Are you relaxed?"

"I'm working on it."

"Anything I can do to help?"

# NINE

CHELSEA FOUND HER razor on the edge of the tub, and resting her leg along the edge, she began to shave. "Isn't it your turn to ask me a question? A *real* question?"

She didn't need to see him to know he was smiling. "Yeah. I guess I can cross 'What are you wearing?' off the list."

"I guess so."

"Maybe you should run more hot water into the tub," he told her. "I wouldn't want you to get cold."

She'd turned off the air-conditioning and opened the windows before she'd run her bathwater. It had to be close to eighty-five degrees in there. A bead of sweat ran down her neck and she used her washcloth to cool herself off. "Believe me, I'm in no danger of getting cold. It's steamy in here."

He drew in another deep breath. "I bet. Yow."

"I'm still waiting for your question."

"My brain is immobilized by the pictures my vivid imagination is creating."

"*I* have a question, then," she said. "I want to know where you learned to kiss."

Johnny laughed. "Would you believe through years of dedicated practice?"

"Yes."

"Actually, when I was seven, my mother and I lived next door to a kid named Howie Bernstein. Howie had a sixteen-year-old sister, and—I can't remember her name, but she used to lecture us on how to kiss a girl. Apparently, she went out with a couple of boys who had no finesse—they did little more than grab and suck, if you know what I mean."

"Oh, I know exactly what you mean." Chelsea closed her eyes, using her hands to rinse the soap from her skin, letting his voice wash over her as well.

"So Howie's sister was determined that Howie not grow up to be an insensitive jerk, so she regularly cornered him—and me with him—and told us that when we kissed a girl, we had to remember to take it *really* slow—even twice as slow as we thought. She said we had to pay attention to little details and take our time. I was only seven, but I can still remember her telling us that. So I guess I owe it all to Howie Bernstein."

"God bless Howie Bernstein's sister, whatever her name is."

"Howie used to call her Butthead, but I know that's not her real name."

"Probably not."

"She was beautiful and funny and smart. I remember wishing I had a sister like her. It got kind of lonely sometimes with just my mother and me."

"What happened to your father?" Chelsea asked.

"He died in Vietnam when I was around three. I never really knew him."

Chelsea closed her eyes. "God, I'm sorry."

"Yeah, me too," Johnny told her. "More now

than I was as a kid. I mean, I grew up in a pretty tough neighborhood, and a lot of kids had dads that beat the crap out of them—so I didn't mind not having a father back then. But when I got older, I could've used having a guy around the house—you know, like a role model. But all I had were the stories my mother used to tell. About how my father wanted to go to college and become a schoolteacher, but his parents died when he was a kid, and he had no money. So he enlisted in the army, thinking he could sign up and serve for a few years and then go to school courtesy of Uncle Sam. He didn't factor dying into the equation."

"How did he die?"

"His transport plane was shot down. According to the stories, he was one of about seventy-five men who survived the crash, but he died trying to pull the pilot out of the plane. It was burning, and they could hear the pilot screaming, and my father was the only one who went in after him. The whole thing went up in a fireball, and they were both killed."

Johnny paused, but Chelsea didn't speak. She sat, watching water drip down the tile walls, trying to imagine *her* father going into a burning plane to try to save the pilot's life. She couldn't picture it—because he'd never do it. Oh, he'd have gone in without batting an eye if his money had been in danger of going up in flames, but not for some stranger.

"But then, after my mother died," Johnny continued, "I was going through some of her papers, sorting things out, you know, and I found my father's army records, along with some letters he wrote to her. It didn't take me long to realize that that story she told me about him wanting money to go to college—that was something of a rather huge white lie. The truth was, he was busted for knocking over a liquor store, and since he was only eighteen and it was his first known offense, he was given a choice: jail or the army. That was right around the time he'd gotten my mother pregnant and married her. He had a wife and kid to think about, so he took his chances in 'Nam. He actually made it through his first tour without even being injured.

"The way I figure it, he came back and kicked around for about a year before he started to get into trouble again—or at least until he started to get caught. This time he served about six months in prison, and when he got out, he reenlisted. I read a letter he wrote to my mother from Walpole right before his release, telling her he didn't know what else he could do besides go back to Vietnam. He couldn't handle the grind of nine to five, and he was a lousy criminal too. The only thing he'd ever been good at was patrolling the jungles of Southeast Asia. So he went back, and he died trying to save some stranger's life. He was the only one who went into the burning plane to help that pilot. The *only* one." He was silent for a moment. "I could never figure out why my mother didn't just tell me the truth."

"Maybe she wanted you to remember him as a hero," Chelsea said softly.

"But that's just it," Johnny said. "Didn't she realize that the truth was better than the story she told? I mean, here's this two-bit criminal, this total screwup of a guy who can't hold a job, who's done hard time in Walpole, and he's the only man—one out of nearly a hundred soldiers—who can't just stand there and listen to another man burn to death. My father didn't go into that plane because he wanted to die. He wasn't trying to be a hero. He probably went in there cursing that pilot to hell and back. But he did go in. He couldn't keep himself from trying to save that guy. Everyone thought he was some good-for-nothing lowlife, but inside, he was a better man than all of them. To me, it makes him even more of a hero, since he wasn't a hero to start with."

"You're right, but I can see it from your mother's point of view too," Chelsea told him. "I could see how she wouldn't want her son growing up knowing his father had done time in prison. Didn't you tell me that she was a doctor?"

"Yeah. She went back to school to get her degree about four years after my dad died. It took her that long to deal with it. My old man may not have been able to hold a job, but he was one of those guys that charmed the socks off of everyone he met. Everybody loved him." Johnny laughed. "My mother had this note written to him by the warden up at Walpole, wishing him the best of luck upon his parole, can you believe it? It was in with his letters and stuff.

"Anyway, she never really got over his death, but she finally reached a point where she had to move forward with her own life. I remember when she sat me down and told me she was going back to college—that she was going for a medical degree. I was eight that year, and she gave me my own key to the apartment, because I was going to have to let myself in after school, while she was in class. That was when I first learned to cook." He laughed. "I had to, or I would've starved to death. My mother almost never got home before eight-thirty for about six years. I started cooking *her* dinner."

"You must've been scared—eight years old and alone for all that time every day."

"I was used to it. It was no big deal."

"When I was twelve, I spent three days totally by myself—and it was a *very* big deal," Chelsea said. "And necessity *wasn't* the mother of invention in my case. I *didn't* learn to cook—I just ate junk food the entire time. You know—and this is something you should know about me, seeing as how I *am* your wife—but I *still* can't cook. I'm the kind of person who can burn water."

"Maybe I could give you a few lessons."

Chelsea closed her eyes, not wanting to think about the kind of lessons she wanted Johnny Anziano to give her. "I don't think so. If I learned how, then I'd have to cook all the time. As it stands, I've got a great reason for ordering takeout."

"I love to cook. I loved it when I was eight too. I'd much rather cook my own dinner than eat out. I'm too critical of other people's cooking."

"Do you really know how to cook?" she asked. "*Really* cook?"

"Isn't it my turn to ask a question?"

"No, I think it's still my turn," she told him, knowing full well that she was wrong.

"No way! You just asked me about fourteen questions in a row," he told her. "It's definitely my turn. And I want to know why you spent three days by yourself when you were twelve."

Chelsea stretched her foot toward the faucet, and with her toe she lifted the toggle that opened the drain, letting some of the cooling water out of the tub. "I was in some really intense negotiations with my parents about trying out for the middle-school field-hockey team. I didn't want to do it because Sierra had played and won Field Hockey Goddess of the East Coast, or some major award like that. The way I saw it, Sierra was Miss Perfect, and this was just going to be another way that I would fail to live up to her glorious standards."

She closed the drain with her toe, but then scooted forward to add more hot water to the tub.

She raised her voice to be heard over the rush of the water. "So after they told me that I *would* play on the team—I didn't have a choice in the matter—I counternegotiated by packing up my things and moving out."

Johnny laughed in surprise. "Are you saying that you ran away from home?"

"Yep. And you want to know the really stupid thing?"

"Oh, yeah," Johnny said. "I get the feeling this is going to be good."

"After I left, nobody missed me."

"You're kidding."

Chelsea shut off the hot water. "Nope. I happened to run away on the weekend of the big Harvard/Yale game. My entire family spent all of Saturday preparing for the game, all of Sunday tailgating in Cambridge, and all of Monday recovering. Everyone just assumed I was home, pouting."

"Where did you go?"

"I drove out to our beach house in Truro—on the Cape."

"You *drove*?"

"Yep. Took Daddy's Jaguar and headed for Cape Cod."

"I'm assuming that wasn't the first time you'd been behind the wheel of a car." Johnny paused. "Of course, I realize that with you, I probably shouldn't assume anything."

"No, you were right the first time. Troy taught me to drive when I was ten. I was kind of like his pet monkey—it amused him to teach me to do all sorts of grown-up things. That same year he tried to get me to drink beer and smoke, too, but I was a smart kid. I hated the taste of beer, and I knew smoking would give me cancer." She swirled the water around in the tub, trying to mix the cool with the hot. "But I *loved* to drive. I had to sit on about three pillows and pull the seat all the way up so I could reach the gas pedal. Troy used to take me out a couple times a week. Sometimes he'd even wake me up in the middle of the night so I could get a chance to drive on the highway without anyone around to see me and call the cops. By the time I was twelve, I was an excellent driver. I'd probably already clocked a few thousand miles."

"Driving, smoking, drinking…I guess what Troy couldn't teach you, his good friend Bent did, huh?" Johnny asked.

"Is that your next question?"

"No, I was just marveling at the irony. So back to this story: You took Daddy's Jag, and you actually made it all the way out to Truro without getting stopped?"

Chelsea put her head back and watched the flickering candlelight reflecting off the moisture-laden walls. "It was off-season. No one gave me a second glance. At least not until I'd been at the beach house for three days. That was when I was nabbed—by a patrol cop who knew there wasn't supposed to be anyone staying at the Spencer cottage that week. He brought me down to the police station and called my parents—who still didn't even know I was gone." She laughed, but there wasn't much humor in it. "What a joke."

"So did you have to play on the field-hockey team?"

"You bet. I was grounded for everything *except* field-hockey practice for three months. It was not a happy year—that was only the first of a long string of power struggles I didn't stand a chance of winning."

"Maybe that's really why you don't want to get married," Johnny suggested. "Because your parents want you to."

"Thank you so much, Dr. Freud. I think *maybe* I'm a little bit more in control of my own life now that I'm twenty-eight years old."

"Ready for my next question?" Johnny was smoothly changing the subject. He was a very smart man.

"Isn't it my turn yet?"

"Nope. If there was one single thing in your life that you could do differently, what would it be?"

Chelsea didn't have to think about that for long. "I wouldn't have had that affair with Benton Scott. Definitely not."

"That wasn't your fault—you were too young," Johnny said. "*He* was the one who should have known better."

"I wasn't too young," Chelsea countered.

"You think sixteen's not too young?"

She hadn't been sixteen, not the second time. Chelsea was silent for a moment, wondering how much to tell him. The truth? Why not? He was her husband, after all. Why not share her darkest, most dreadful secret with him?

She moistened her suddenly dry lips, wondering what he was going to say. "I wasn't talking about the first time I had an affair with Bent," she said.

"I was talking about the second. After he was married."

Johnny was noticeably quiet.

"It was about five years ago," she went on, "and I was working for my master's degree. I hadn't seen Bent in years, and I ran into him downtown. He looked almost exactly the same. It was weird, as if he'd time-warped through the past seven years. He told me he and his family had just moved to a house out in one of the W suburbs—Weston or Wayland or Wellesley, I don't remember which. But because they weren't living in town anymore, he'd gotten a small apartment near the courthouse for the times when he had trials and he wanted to stay overnight . . . and you know exactly where this is leading, right?"

"Yeah."

"Disappointed in me?"

"Yeah."

Chelsea squeezed her eyes shut. "Do you hate me now?"

"Of course not. Hell, everyone makes mistakes."

"It wasn't as tawdry as I've made it sound," she told him. "I didn't go to his apartment with him right away—not for a few weeks, anyway. But he started calling me regularly, and we had lunch, and then dinner, and then..." She closed her eyes again, wondering what Johnny was really thinking. Sure, everyone made mistakes, but she'd knowingly slept with a married man. It had not been her finest moment.

"It *was* tawdry," she admitted. "Unbearably tawdry. I only went there once, but once is enough, isn't it? I guess I did it mostly to get back at Nicole—Bent's wife. But she probably never knew, and *I* was the one who felt like crap afterward. Of course, it didn't help matters that I was still in love with the bastard." She took a deep breath. "So there it is. The one thing I'd do *much* differently if I could only do it over."

"Maybe your mistake was in letting yourself fall in love with a man like Bent in the first place," Johnny said quietly.

Chelsea snorted. "Yeah, like we can control who we fall in love with?" She sat up, letting the water out of the tub. "I'm turning into a prune. I've got to get out of here." She stood up and stepped out of the tub.

"Are you still in love with him?"

His words stopped her. "I don't know," she

admitted. "I...haven't been with that many men, if you want to know the truth. And I haven't been with anybody who made me feel even close to the way Bent did." Except Johnny. Those kisses Johnny had given her had been totally off the scale.

"That sounds like a challenge to me." His voice was as soft as the towel she reached for to dry herself with.

"Well, it's not. I don't want to be someone's challenge, or someone's prize or someone's bonus or—"

"How about someone's partner?"

"There's no such thing as a true partnership," she told him as she dried herself off. "Someone always has more power. In everything from a business deal to a love affair. There's always someone who wants more. And if you want something—or someone—too badly, you're definitely in the weaker position." Chelsea hung her towel up and reached for the moisturizing lotion on the counter next to the sinks. "That's what happened with me and Bent—the first time around, I mean. I wanted to go out with this exciting, handsome, grown-up man—enough to get myself involved in a sexual relationship that I probably wasn't ready for. And I ended up losing more than I bargained for—my trust and innocence as well as my virginity. I've been careful ever since then never to want anyone that much."

She tucked the phone between her shoulder and her chin as she squeezed some of the fragrant lotion into her hand. "Of course, that's not so hard—I just compare anyone I meet to Bent. He was a remarkably talented lover. And I don't necessarily mean in the physical sense, although he was no slouch in that department either. But I'm talking about presentation."

"Presentation?"

"Yeah, he was romantic. He would take me places, treat me like an adult, order me champagne or wine with dinner. He took me to fancy hotels, treated me as if I were special. And for someone who was so damned selfish, he spent a huge amount of time *giving* pleasure. Sometimes I wish . . ."

"What?" Johnny's word was as soft as a breath.

She hesitated.

"Tell me what you wish."

"Sometimes I wish I could have a physical relationship of that intensity now. At the time I didn't fully appreciate it."

"You can, you know." His voice was just a whisper, just a caress. "*We* can."

What was she doing, discussing the intimacies of her past sexual experiences with Johnny. Talk about playing with fire. "I should go. It's getting late—we should both be in bed."

Johnny didn't say anything right away, and Chelsea felt her words seem to echo across the line: *we should be in bed.*

When he finally spoke, his voice was hoarse. "We should definitely be in bed. Together. I think you probably know that I've been sitting here, listening to you take your bath, listening to you talk about your first lover, imagining the way you must look lying back in that tub—" He broke off, swearing softly. "I wasn't going to say anything like this, but as long as I've started, I've got to tell you that I've been sitting here, wishing to God that I could walk in there, climb into that tub with you, and make you forget Benton Scott's name. I want you so bad, Chelsea, I may not live through the night."

His words sent a wave of desire pulsating through her, heat pooling sharply in her belly and between her legs. She gazed at herself in the mirror, at all that bare skin reflecting the flickering candlelight. Her hair was slicked back, her face clean of makeup, making her look like a stranger. A naked stranger. A stranger who didn't need to be careful about wanting someone too much.

"I wish I could show you," Johnny murmured. "I wish I could walk into your room and show you just how much I want you."

Chelsea gazed at the stranger in the mirror, who was gazing back at her. Her breasts were peaked with desire, her nipples tautly erect, enticingly sensitized, so that even the slight breeze blowing in through the open window was enough to make her shiver.

She could remember how it felt—the excitement, the need, of wanting something she knew she shouldn't have. She remembered the total release of letting that wanting consume her completely.

"I want you, too, John," she whispered, watching the woman in the mirror rub lotion down her arms and across her breasts.

Johnny drew in a ragged breath at her words. "Damn, I want to touch you."

"I want you to touch me too." In the mirror, the stranger's chest was rising and falling rapidly with every breath she took. And then she was sixteen again. Sixteen, and recklessly carefree. Now was all that mattered. Feeling good right *now*. She could barely believe the words that came out of her mouth. "John. We could unlock the door." The door that adjoined their two rooms. They each could unbolt it from their own side, and...

His voice vibrated with his intensity. "Are you sure you want to do that?"

She didn't hesitate. She only wanted. "Yes."

He laughed, a short burst of amazement and disbelief. "Wow. You sound...convinced."

"I am. Right now. But don't make me think too hard about it."

He took a deep breath. "I do want you to think hard about it. You made me promise—"

Chelsea didn't want to think about legal complications. The naked stranger in the mirror wouldn't give such things a second thought. Nor would her sixteen-year-old self. "I don't care. I want you more than I've ever wanted anybody."

He was silent for a moment. "Are you serious?" When he spoke, his voice was thick with his own desire.

"Meet me at the door, okay?"

"More than Bent?" he asked, then quickly added, "Forget I asked that. I shouldn't have asked you that."

"Yes." She answered him anyway. "More than Bent. Meet me at the door, John. Please?"

"Oh, God," he breathed, then took a deep breath. "Chelsea, I *promised* you we wouldn't do this." He took another deep breath. "Okay," he said.

"Okay?"

"No! Not okay, I'll meet you at the door. I meant, okay, I've figured out what we can . . . Look, just listen to me, all right?"

"I'm listening."

"Put down the phone and go into the bedroom, and pick up the extension that's next to the bed, okay? Then go and hang up the bathroom line. I'll meet you back in your bed."

"Don't I have to unlock the—"

"No," he said. "You don't. Just do what I said, all right?"

Johnny took a fortifying swallow out of one of the bottles of beer he'd ordered more than an hour ago from room service as he waited for Chelsea to come back to the phone.

He stood up and paced, carrying the phone with him, and he found himself standing in the bedroom doorway, staring out into the darkened living room, at the private door that connected their two suites.

Chelsea wanted him. She wanted him to walk through that connecting door and make love to her. She was his wife, he was her husband. They were legally wed.

So what the hell was he doing, standing over here?

He wanted her so badly, he was in serious pain.

If she wanted him even half as much, she would be dying for his touch—just as he was dying for hers. He wished he had the strength to go through those doors and make love to her only with his hands and his mouth, but he knew if he got near her he wouldn't be able to resist loving her completely. Those words he'd spoken in the restaurant were the truth. He wouldn't be strong enough to stop himself from making love to her.

And if he did that, he would be breaking the promise he'd made to her. And tomorrow, when she woke up, the impact of what they'd done

*Suzanne Brockmann*

would fracture the growing friendship between them, possibly destroying it beyond repair.

And he wouldn't do that. He couldn't.

The truth was, he liked her. A lot. Enough to want more than just one night of incredible sex.

Enough maybe even to want a lifetime.

The thought caught him off guard, and he shook his head, pushing it away. He refused to think that way. Not about a woman who so clearly didn't want *anyone* around forever.

"John?" Chelsea was back on the phone, her voice slightly breathless.

"I'm here," he told her, turning his back on that door, walking back toward his bed.

"I know," she said, her slightly husky voice thickened with desire. "But I want you over *here*."

"Lie down and close your eyes," he told her. He could hear her pulling back the bedcovers, hear the rustling of the sheets. "Are your eyes closed?"

"Yes."

"You know I can't really be with you tonight, Chelsea," he said quietly. "Not if I want to keep the promise I made to you. But you know I'd knock down this wall to get to you if I could."

"John—"

"Shh. Just listen. Because the day that annulment comes through, well, I'm probably going to have to work that night, but after work, I'm going to come over to your place. I'll have a key to let myself in, because by the time I get there, it's going to be pretty late. You'll be in bed already, just like you are right now. Maybe you'll even be asleep."

"No, I won't." Chelsea spoke with such certainty. "I'll be waiting for you."

"You're naked under the sheets," Johnny told her, letting himself lie back on his bed, his feet still on the floor. If he closed his eyes, he could picture her all too clearly. "And I still have all my clothes on. I just stand there for a minute, looking down at you, you looking up at me, both of us knowing exactly what's going to happen next."

"And then I pull back the sheet," Chelsea said.

Johnny smiled. He hadn't been sure at first if she would be willing to play along, or if she'd simply want to listen to him talk. But it didn't surprise him that she'd want to take an active part in this game. He felt a rush of heat and desire at the thought of her lying in her bed, willing to let him guide her so intimately.

"I'm still standing there, looking at you in the

moonlight. God! You're so beautiful. I can't believe you're going to share yourself with me."

"I sit up and reach for you...."

Johnny groaned at the powerful visual images in his head. "I can't keep from touching you any longer. So I sit down next to you, and I kiss you. Your skin is so soft and smooth—I'm touching you everywhere—I can't get enough. Your back, your arms, your throat, your breasts—they fit in my hands so perfectly. Do you feel me touching you? You have to help me a little bit here, Chelsea. Can you do that?"

"Yes."

She was breathing harder, and he was too. Because now he had the fantasy *and* the reality to think about, and both were overwhelmingly erotic. He'd never done anything even remotely like this before. He'd never been one to spend time on words and talking when it came to making love. But right now all he could give Chelsea were his words and his voice. He was determined to give her as much pleasure as he could, and the words seemed to flow.

"I want to taste you, and you want it, too, so I do. I touch the very tip of your breast with my tongue, very lightly—just a little. And then I look at you to see if you like the way that feels."

"Oh, yes," she breathed. "I like that."

"So I do it again, and this time you want more, so you push yourself up, up into my mouth, and I *really* love that. And now I've got you in my mouth, sucking and pulling, tugging at you, and you taste so good, I think I'm gonna die...."

"I want to take your clothes off," Chelsea said, surprising him again by taking the lead. "Your clothes are getting in the way. I unfasten your jeans, pull down the zipper—it's not easy to pull it down because you're...you're so hard."

The sound of her voice, whispering those words in his ear was mind-blowing. "I am," Johnny said, and it was true. "Chelsea, I am *so* hot for you...."

He wanted her—in every way imaginable. He wanted to walk into a crowded room and know he'd find her waiting for him, smiling as he came closer, her smile telling of secrets shared and promises made. *Do you take this woman...?* Yes. Yes, he wanted to take her—and keep her. He wanted to make love to her, and to love her.

To love her...God help him, he was falling in love with his wife.

"You help me push down your jeans," she murmured into his ear, "and God, you're not wearing any shorts. There's just your jeans...and you. I touch you, my fingers against your skin—do you feel me touching you?"

"Chelsea—"

"And then you reach for me, too, touching me...."

She moaned, and Johnny could barely speak.

"Chelsea," was all he managed to say.

"Yes...?"

Somehow, he had to get back into control. Somehow, he took a deep breath and brought the focus back to her. "I'm touching you," he rasped. "You're so soft...and hot. So smooth, like silk. I touch you lightly at first, then harder. Deeper."

"Yeah..."

"It feels so good—you touching me that way"— his voice sounded harsh in his own ears, rough from his desire—"and me touching you. You push your hips up, against me—you want more."

"Yeah..."

"And I want to get inside of you—"

"You are," she said. "You're on top of me, and

you're inside me, and it feels *so good,* and we're moving together and oh, John—"

He heard her cry out, and it pushed him over the edge. He heard her drop the phone, heard it bounce along the floor, heard it rocking slightly before coming to a rest.

And then there was silence. One minute stretched into two, two into three.

"Chelsea?" Johnny said when he could finally speak. "Are you all right?"

He heard a rustling sound, and then a scraping as the phone was probably pulled along the tile floor by its cord.

Then: "Hello?" She sounded out of breath.

"Hi," Johnny said. "Are you okay?"

She laughed. "Yeah. I'm...extremely okay."

He had to know. "Did you just...?"

"Yeah," she said. "Did you?"

"Yeah," he admitted. "I wasn't exactly planning to, but..."

"Oh, my God," she said. "We just had phone sex."

"It beats a cold shower," he said. "No pun intended."

Chelsea laughed. But when she spoke her voice

was softer. "What do you say to someone after you've had phone sex with them?"

"I don't know," Johnny admitted. "This is a first for me too."

"You're kidding. You must be a natural."

"Oh, man, if anyone's a natural, it's you. You could make a fortune on one of those 900 lines."

"No, thanks. I prefer the real thing."

"Be patient. That'll come in just a few more days."

He could hear her smile. "No pun intended?"

Johnny smiled too. "No pun intended."

He heard her sigh, heard the rustle of her sheets. "I really like you, John Anziano," she said. "I can't wait to jump your bones for real."

He had to laugh. "I'm looking forward to that too—especially when you put it so romantically."

"Good night, John."

"Good night." Johnny heard the click as the connection was cut. "I think I'm in love with you, Chelsea," he added, knowing that he'd never dare say the words aloud if she were listening.

# TEN

CHELSEA SAT IN the early-morning rush hour, waiting for the light to turn green, knowing that she had allowed herself more than enough time to battle the traffic and find a parking spot before her eight-thirty appointment with her lawyer. Shoot, she had enough time to leave her car right here and *walk* the last few miles to Tim von Reuter's office, if need be.

No, the butterflies in her stomach weren't from fear of being late. They weren't even in anticipation of finally receiving the money from her grandfather's trust.

They were from the thought of seeing Johnny again.

Johnny...

The driver behind her hit his horn, startling her out of her reverie and she put her car into gear and lurched forward through the green light.

It was hard to believe that just yesterday she and Johnny had been in St. Thomas. And the night before last...

God, she couldn't let her mind stray in that direction. The thought of what she'd done—what *they'd* done—still made her cheeks heat with a blush. God, who would've ever thought she could feel the things that she'd felt?

Johnny had called her late the next morning, and she'd felt tongue-tied, almost shy. But he said nothing about the night before as if he'd known she'd be too embarrassed to speak of it. He'd simply been himself—friendly, funny, and impossibly attractive.

They had only one more short day on the island—their flight was scheduled to leave just before sunset. He'd asked her to spend the afternoon with him, and she'd hesitated until he suggested they go into town and explore the port of Charlotte Amalie. He told her he thought it would be smart if they were careful only to go where they were sure there would be crowds.

In other words, no deserted beaches, no out-of-the-way scenic lookouts, and definitely no meeting *anywhere* remotely near their hotel rooms.

Chelsea had put away her laptop and briefcase and had gone with him, and it had been very strange indeed. She'd met him in the lobby—his idea—and when she stepped out of the elevator and met his eyes from all the way across the room, her heart had very nearly stopped beating.

She could see his desire, his wanting, his *need* for her in his dark brown eyes. She felt nearly scalded just from looking at him, and she wondered if everything she wanted, everything she felt, was as transparent.

They'd taken a shuttle into town and wandered through narrow streets and alleyways filled with brightly colored shops and markets. St. Thomas was a duty-free port, famous for its bargains and exotic merchandise, but Chelsea couldn't remember much of what she saw. She'd been aware only of Johnny, of him watching her, wanting her, always careful never to get too close.

He'd made a point not to touch her, not even to brush his hand against hers. He didn't speak of it, but she knew he was as aware as she was that even holding hands would have been too much. Their desire was far too volatile.

Later, on the plane back to Boston, Chelsea had pretended to read, aware of Johnny watching her for the entire flight. Even his five-thousand-watt smile wasn't enough to mask the heat in his eyes.

In Boston, they'd taken separate taxis to their separate homes. But Johnny had called her later, to make sure she'd gotten home safely, and to say good night. Again, they'd stayed up for several hours, talking—about books, movies, music. Talking about everything and anything that popped into their heads. Their tastes didn't always agree and they'd argued good-naturedly more than once.

It was odd, when they'd spent the day together, Chelsea had to search for things to say. But on the phone she felt safe. Relaxed. Well, almost relaxed. There was always an undercurrent of danger as she constantly wondered if and when they were going to talk about what they'd done the night before.

Johnny had told her things about himself that she hadn't known. He played jazz clarinet, and on his nights off, he often sat in with the house band at a club near his apartment downtown. He also had a black belt in karate. She'd seen evidence of that the first day they'd met, when he'd made short work of the gang of kids who'd snatched her purse.

Chelsea, in turn, had found herself telling him things she'd never told anyone—about how much it hurt to be labeled the family's black sheep, about how, no matter what she did, she couldn't seem to win her father's respect. About how she wasn't even sure she *wanted* the respect of a man like her father—with his preference for money and business above all else, with his prejudices and narrow-minded way of thinking.

Johnny had listened, letting her talk, as if he were somehow aware that this was not something she shared with just anyone.

They'd said good night at close to four in the morning, without having mentioned their encounter from the night before even once. Which was a good thing, because Chelsea wasn't quite sure what to say.

Except to break down and confess to him that she wanted him so badly that she couldn't eat or sleep or even think straight.

Chelsea tried to count the number of days before she could start the legal proceedings necessary for the annulment. She didn't know precisely how long the process took. She promised herself to make a point of talking to Tim von Reuter about it this morning. She'd also ask him about the logistics of a divorce. It was her understanding that a divorce—even an amicable one—was both time-consuming and costly.

She turned down Newbury Street and pulled into the entrance of the parking lot on the corner of Clarendon. She took the receipt the attendant handed her, and leaving her keys in the ignition, she grabbed her briefcase and her jacket and got out of the car.

And ran directly into Johnny.

"Whoa!" he said, then, "Hey, hi!" in recognition. He'd put his arms around her to steady her, but he didn't take them away.

She'd forgotten how tall he was, how broad his shoulders were, how hard his muscles were. Her breasts were pressed tightly against his chest, her hips locked against his. And still he didn't let her go.

"Good morning," she whispered, aware that

she was gazing up at him like a complete fool. She would have been absolutely unable to move even if he had released her.

He was wearing a gray suit today, in honor of the meeting at the lawyer's, no doubt. His shirt was a lighter shade of gray, his tie slightly darker. It was a style of fashion that she hadn't particularly liked before, but on Johnny, it looked wonderful.

He was gazing back at her with that now-familiar molten heat in his eyes getting stronger by the second. She could feel his arousal, instant and unmistakable against the softness of her stomach, and she felt her insides flip-flop as if she were experiencing zero gravity.

"Oh, damn," Johnny whispered, his gaze locked onto her mouth as if he were hypnotized. And then he kissed her.

It was a kiss of pure desire, of near-delirious need. Chelsea dropped her briefcase as she kissed him back with the same fierce hunger. They were standing on the sidewalk, with pedestrians heading for work streaming past them, and they were kissing passionately, as if no one and nothing else existed in the world.

She felt his hands sweep down her back to cup

her rear end, pulling her even more possessively against him, even as his tongue claimed her mouth.

Chelsea experienced instant nuclear meltdown. Her bones turned to jelly and her blood turned to fire.

And she knew in that moment that if there were ever a man she'd want to be possessed by in every awful, nonfeminist, unliberated sense of the word, it was this man. She was ready to do anything to keep this kiss from ending. She was ready to give up her plans for a simple annulment. She was ready to sign on to be his slave or to sell her soul simply to keep him near her.

He made a tortured sound deep in the back of his throat that made her wonder if maybe he wasn't ready to do the same.

It was insane. She'd sworn to herself she'd never let a man control her in any way, shape, or form. Yet here she was, ready to ruin all of her careful plans. Here she was, kissing this man as if there were no tomorrow, right on the sidewalk on Newbury Street.

He pulled back as if it had taken everything he had and then some to stop kissing her. "Chelsea..."

He was breathing hard, his eyes faintly wild as he held her stiffly at arm's length.

"John, will you get a cup of coffee and a bagel with me after we meet with Tim?" she asked him.

It was not the question he'd expected, and she could see from his expression that it threw him slightly, coming off of that kiss. But she hadn't known what else to say. She couldn't ask him simply to rush home with her to consummate their marriage immediately after the meeting with the lawyer, could she? If they were going to take actions that would require a more complicated and involved legal proceeding to end their mock marriage, they'd need to talk about it first, wouldn't they?

And maybe, between now and then, this insanity that possessed her would subside and she'd awaken to find herself back in control of her life, instead of being tossed about like a mindless piece of cork in a stormy sea of sexual desires and fantasies.

"Um, yeah," he said. "Coffee." He let go of her arms, raking his hair back with a hand that was shaking slightly before turning to pick her briefcase up from the sidewalk. "Bagel. Sure. We better... We better get to that meeting, though... now... don't you think?"

Chelsea looked at her watch. They had a little time, but it definitely wasn't enough for them to dash down to Arlington Street and get a room at the fancy Ritz-Carlton Hotel. And that was a *good* thing, she tried to convince herself. "We're a few minutes early. We don't have to rush."

He carried her briefcase as they started down Newbury Street. He was doing his best to pretend that kiss hadn't totally turned him upside down, but Chelsea knew better. It had turned *her* upside down, so much so that she couldn't think about much else besides kissing him again.

And why shouldn't she kiss him again? After all, they had *some* time, but not enough to do anything too outrageous....

She slipped her hand into the crook of his arm, and she could feel the sudden tension in his muscles. He looked at her and shook his head.

"Chelsea, if you want me to try to keep my hands off of you, that's not the way to—"

"We have eleven minutes before we're scheduled to meet with Tim," she told him. "We could either spend it in the waiting room with Mrs. Mert, or we could...do something else with our time. And our hands."

Johnny turned and met her eyes and she could see his surprise as he hesitated.

"Now it's ten minutes and fifteen seconds," she told him, glancing again at her watch. "Are you going to kiss me again, or what?"

He laughed aloud, but he didn't pull her into his arms. Instead, he took a quick look around at the stores and buildings that lined the street. Then he moved swiftly, taking her by the hand and pulling her with him into the entrance of one of the brownstone buildings. The door was locked, but it was recessed from the sidewalk, offering some privacy from the people passing by. He pulled her with him into the corner, near a row of apartment mailboxes, dropped her briefcase on the tile floor, and smiled into her eyes.

"Okay, now ask me that again."

She was lost in his eyes, her fingers sunk into the darkness of the hair that curled around his neck. "Will you kiss me?" Her voice was barely a whisper.

"Absolutely," he said. Then slowly, so slowly, he leaned forward, searching her eyes, his smile fading as he got closer.

Each heartbeat seemed an eternity, but finally his lips brushed hers impossibly gently.

He closed his eyes then, his lashes long and dark against his cheeks as he kissed her again.

Chelsea closed her eyes, too, and allowed herself to luxuriate in the sheer sweetness of Johnny's lips.

He pulled her to him, her body fitting against his as if they had both been made with each other in mind. His hands swept down her back as he kissed her harder, deeper, the sweetness now laced with searing flame.

He lifted his head then, showering kisses on her cheeks, her nose, her eyes, her neck, in between the words he spoke. "I guess you figured ten minutes wasn't enough time to get a room at the Ritz."

Chelsea had to laugh. That was exactly what she had been thinking.

"You told me last night that Tim has to leave for court by nine forty-five," Johnny murmured. "You said we can't be late for this meeting. That's why I got down here so early."

"I'm so glad you were early."

He pulled back to look into her eyes, and he didn't try to hide the flurry of emotions that crossed his face. "You really are, aren't you?"

This time she kissed him, her arms sliding up underneath his suit jacket, the crisp cotton of his shirt a poor substitute for the sensation she truly wanted—the feel of his skin beneath her hands. Still, she loved touching the powerful muscles of his back and she kissed him harder, wishing he could climb inside her mind and experience the pleasure he gave her with just a kiss.

She explored lower and she felt the leather of his belt and then the perfect curve of his derriere beneath the light wool of his pants. She knew this was neither the time nor the place for what she wanted, but she pulled him even closer to her anyway.

He seemed to explode at her touch, and he pressed her against the mailboxes, the solidity of his thigh firmly between her legs. He took control of the kiss, his tongue claiming her mouth as his. His hand swept between them, along the soft silk of her shirt, across her breasts, caressing her, possessing her. His touch was as proprietary as his kisses. He didn't doubt the fact that she belonged to him—every last inch of her.

She did belong to him.

The thought alarmed her, and Chelsea pulled back, suddenly frightened at the intensity of the way this man made her feel.

Johnny felt her hesitation and made himself back away from her. Leaning on the other side of the entryway with his back to her, bracing himself with both hands against the wall, he tried to steady his ragged breathing.

"I can't go for coffee with you after this meeting," he told her. "Because I want a whole hell of a lot more than a bagel."

Chelsea rested her forehead against the cold metal of the mailboxes. "I do too," she whispered, forcing herself to acknowledge the truth. "I want more too."

He turned and looked at her. "Your problem is that there's a difference between what you think you want...and what you want." He laughed painfully, running his hands down his face. "Or maybe that's *my* problem, huh?"

"I do know what I want," she said quietly.

He pushed himself forward, off the wall. "I know. You want the money from your grandfather's trust. It's time—let's go get it."

Johnny straightened his clothes, then grabbed her briefcase.

Chelsea gazed at him, unable to speak. He was wrong. She knew what she wanted. She wanted

Johnny. She wanted him to go home with her after the meeting. She wanted him to be her lover. She wanted him to belong to her as surely as she was his. But she couldn't say the words aloud.

Instead she fixed her hair and followed Johnny back into the harsh glare of the morning sunlight.

As Johnny watched, the Ice Princess made an appearance for the first time in days.

"I beg your pardon?" Chelsea said to Tim von Reuter. "The first payment is only one hundred dollars, and I won't receive the second payment until I've been married for *how* long?"

"One year." The lawyer sat behind his desk, clearly unhappy with the news he'd given her. "There was nothing in the description of this trust fund that led me to believe it wasn't set up identically to the funds your grandfather left for your brother and sister and your cousins, which allowed them to receive the money directly following their wedding."

"Yet now you're telling me that it's different. *My* trust was set up entirely differently. How could you not have known?"

Von Reuter was definitely starting to get a bad case of frostbite from Chelsea's chilly gaze. "You saw me break the seal on the envelope," he told her. "This is as much of a surprise to me as it is to you."

"Can we contest this? Challenge it in some way?"

The lawyer shook his head, gesturing with the document that had been in the sealed envelope. "The terms of the trust fund are in writing. It's been signed and witnessed. This is the way your grandfather wanted it, this is what you're going to have to do if you want this money."

"May I?" Johnny asked, reaching for the papers in question. He skimmed them quickly, trying to get past all the wheretofores and thereupons. Von Reuter was right. Amid all the legal mumbo jumbo, Chelsea's grandfather's wishes regarding the money were as clear as day. Chelsea was to receive only a paltry hundred dollars from the trust until her first anniversary.

He looked up to find her gazing out the window, distant and untouchable. She glanced in his direction. "He knew," she said, more to herself than to him. "He knew I'd never willingly get married. He knew I'd try to cheat the rules."

To his surprise, despite the fact that she'd tried to hide behind her Ice Princess facade, her eyes filled with tears.

And when she spoke, her words surprised him. "God, I miss that nasty old man. He always swore he'd get back at me for all those times I beat him at chess." She laughed, one fat tear escaping down her cheek. "I guess this is his idea of a good joke."

"The good news is that he left you nearly eight times the amount he left your brothers and sisters," Von Reuter told her.

*Eight* times? Johnny flipped to the back of the document and there was the amount of money that had been placed in trust for Chelsea. That money, combined with the interest it would have made all these years, was the equivalent of winning the lottery. Chelsea would be set for life.

"Screw the money. I don't want the money. If I can't get to it now, it doesn't do me any good." Chelsea stood up, wiping her face. "How long will it take to get this marriage annulled?"

It was obviously not a question Tim von Reuter had been expecting. "Why don't we finish talking about the ramifications of this trust before we—"

"I want to talk about the annulment now. How long will it take?"

Von Reuter shifted uncomfortably in his seat. "Well, that depends on a lot of different variables...."

Chelsea swore, leaning over his desk almost threateningly. "If you don't know, will you *please* just say you don't know?"

The lawyer nearly choked on the words. "I don't know."

There was a note of desperation in her voice. "Give it your best guess, Tim. Please?"

"Best-case scenario? I know we'll need to schedule a court date.... Maybe a month?"

Chelsea seemed to crumble, holding on to the edge of the desk. "Oh, my God. *That* long?"

Johnny stood up. "Lookit, Chelsea, I know you're disappointed, and I know that you don't want to be married to me for even one second longer than you have to, but a month's really not that much time in the grand scheme of things."

"Oh, John, no—you don't understand." She turned to face him, her blue eyes enormous in her face. "This doesn't have to do with me not wanting to be married. This is about not wanting to wait a whole month to"—she glanced almost furtively at Von Reuter and lowered her voice—"to be with you."

Johnny nearly staggered from the impact of her words. She was upset, *incredibly* upset, because she didn't want to have to wait an entire month to make love to him. His heart was in his throat. "So we'll have to get a divorce. Big deal."

She shook her head. "Without that money, I probably couldn't afford a divorce. *Everything* I've got is tied up in my business. I haven't even made the mortgage payments on my condo for the past three months." She looked as if she were about to burst into tears.

Johnny turned to Von Reuter. "Tim, is there somewhere Chelsea and I can talk privately?"

The lawyer stood up. "Use my office. Please. If you'll excuse me?"

Johnny waited until the door closed behind Von Reuter. Then he turned to Chelsea. "Here's what we're going to do, okay? We're going to stay married for a year. After that you'll be able to afford all the divorces you want."

She stared at him in total disbelief. "You'd do that? For an *entire* year?"

"Let's see, an entire year, married to the most beautiful, incredible woman I've ever met?" he asked, pretending to consider it. "Somehow I'll suffer through."

He couldn't tell if she was going to laugh or cry.

She took a deep breath and did neither. "So what's your cut?"

Johnny shook his head, not understanding. "My cut?"

"Yeah. What percentage do you want?"

"Percentage?"

"Of the money."

Johnny didn't want a percentage. The money was the last thing he'd been thinking about. But letting her think he was in this for the money was better than telling her the truth and scaring her to death. He shrugged. "I don't know. Ten percent?"

"That's *all*?"

"Ten percent of the money waiting for you in that trust fund is nothing to sneeze at."

"I'll give you twenty-five percent."

He had to laugh. "If this is the way you negotiate, no wonder your business is short of funds."

"We're talking about a solid year of your life—I still can't believe you would do this for me."

"In case you haven't noticed, I kind of like you," he told her. "I asked you out first, remember?"

"You asked me to go to dinner," she reminded him. "Not to marry you for a year."

"If my choice was between zero or three hundred and sixty-five dinners, I'd take the three sixty-five."

Chelsea's eyes were filled with tears again.

"I get more than the money for doing this, you know," he continued softly. "If we're going to be married for a year, we're going to be *married* for a year. Starting tonight, you'll be my wife. For real."

She took a tissue from a box near Von Reuter's desk and wiped her eyes and nose. "Only starting tonight?"

Johnny checked his watch, dizzy from the possibilities. But it was nearly nine-thirty. They still had to talk to Tim, tell him what they planned to do, make sure there were no loopholes they'd overlooked. Even if that took only five minutes—and it would surely take longer—that still left them only an hour. And an hour wasn't long enough to do what he wanted to do. He swore softly.

"I promised my boss I'd be at work by ten-thirty," he told her.

"I thought you worked in the evenings."

"I do. Mostly. But there's a private party that starts at four, and he's counting on me to be in early to help prepare."

She was looking at him as if he were one of his gourmet dinners. "I don't want to wait," she said suddenly.

He didn't want to, either. The thought suddenly occurred to him that they could lock Von Reuter's office door and get it on right there on the lawyer's desk. But as appealing a thought as that was, he knew he didn't want to make love to Chelsea that way for the first time. He didn't want to rush. He wanted to take his sweet time.

"Since the party starts early, it'll end early," he promised her. "I'll be home by ten."

Home. "Where do you live?" she asked. "God, I don't even know where you live."

"I have a condo near the harbor, but...why don't I just plan to come out to your place." He smiled. "As a matter of fact, why don't you give me a key?"

# ELEVEN

"So you think with today's market, we can list it at five hundred K?" Chelsea asked, making a note on her pad as she spoke on the phone.

"I would even try five twenty-five," the real-estate agent told her. "In that building, in that part of town, with two bathrooms and all those renovations you've done . . . For the type of upscale condominium that you have, it's definitely a seller's market."

"But I need to sell it fast," Chelsea said. "Immediately. As in, the day before yesterday."

She did the math on her notepad for both

numbers, figuring in the agent's commission, the closing costs, the amount of equity she had, minus the last few mortgage payments she'd missed and the ensuing penalties. If she sold the place for five hundred thousand, she'd walk away with just under forty thousand, of which she'd have to pay about half in taxes. But if she wanted to *sell* for five hundred, she'd have to list it higher. . . .

"Let's go with five hundred twenty-five," she told the agent. "How soon can you get it listed?"

"I'll messenger the paperwork to your office for you to sign. And I'll put the listing in the MLS computer this afternoon," he said. "We'll have to set up a time for the agents in my office to see the unit."

"The sooner the better," Chelsea told him. "You set it up—I'll adjust my schedule to fit yours."

As she hung up the phone she looked up to see Moira standing in her doorway.

"I can't believe you're really going to do it," her friend said. "You're selling your condo and moving in with a guy named Giovanni Anziano."

"I'm selling my condo to make the first payment of the loan," Chelsea reminded her.

Moira sat down across from her, resting her

elbows on the edge of Chelsea's desk and her chin in her hands. "Do your parents know?"

"That I'm selling my condo? No. I just made that decision."

"I'm not talking about the condo," Moira said. "I'm talking about the truck driver. Do your parents know that the guy you married isn't descended from Italian royalty?"

"John's not a truck driver," Chelsea said. "He works in a restaurant...or something."

"He's a waiter? That'll go over almost as well."

"He's not a waiter," Chelsea said. "At least I don't think so. I think he's some kind of assistant cook...or something." She didn't know. In all of the conversations she'd had with Johnny, she hadn't asked him what, specifically, he did at the restaurant downtown. God, she couldn't even remember the restaurant's name. Had he even told her?

"Your parents are going to have a cow." Moira was grinning. "Can I be there when you tell them?"

"Even if he *is* a waiter, there's nothing wrong with that," Chelsea said, defending Johnny. "He's not going to be a waiter forever—he wants to open his own restaurant."

"With your money, I bet."

"No, with his *share* of the trust fund."

"Relax, I'm just teasing."

Chelsea forced a smile, but truth was, her friend's teasing hit too close to home. Johnny *was* getting paid for the favor he was doing for her. But really, did she honestly expect that he'd agree to stay married to her for an entire year and *not* get paid?

"On an entirely different note," Moira told her, "there was a nifty little stash of crack vials and needles in the doorway when I came in this morning. I talked to Sylvia—you know, the woman who works over at H&R Block—and she gave me some special trash containers marked 'Biohazardous Waste,' that her office gets from the board of health."

"You need to be *really* careful when you pick up those needles," Chelsea said.

"No kidding. But as I was out there, being really careful, it occurred to me that we may want to find a location for our office that doesn't double as a nightly hangout for addicts."

"Moira, God, you know we can't afford to

move. Right now we can't even pay the rent on *this* place!"

Moira pushed herself out of her chair. "I know." She shook her head. "Do you think Sears sells needle-proof gloves?"

"Tomorrow, I'll pick up the trash," Chelsea told her.

"You mean, the biohazardous waste." Moira turned back to look through the doorway. "You know, the sad part of what you just said is that we both know there most likely will be vials and needles there again tomorrow."

Chelsea pressed her forehead against her palms. Damn, she needed cash, and she needed it fast.

But what she really needed was Johnny.

She longed to hear his voice and she nearly picked up the phone and called him at work. But wanting to hear his voice didn't seem like a good enough excuse to call him—and certainly one she'd have trouble admitting.

She glanced at her watch. It was only two o'clock. Would this day never end? The phone rang, and she scooped it up, hoping that it was Johnny.

It wasn't. It was the real-estate agent again. "I

just spoke to some of the people in my office about setting up a realtors' open house at your condo," he told her, "and I found out if we don't do it first thing tomorrow, it won't happen until next Wednesday at the earliest."

"First thing as in what time?" Chelsea asked. She had plans for the morning. They involved sleeping late, breakfast in bed...and Johnny.

"Seven-thirty."

She cringed. "Can't you do it later? Say, noon?"

"Not tomorrow. If you want, we could set it up for next Wednesday at noon."

"Wait. No," Chelsea said. "Go back to tomorrow at seven-thirty. Do I have to be there?"

"Absolutely not."

"In that case, it's fine. I'll send over a key with the paperwork."

Chelsea hung up the phone and glanced at her watch: 2:07. Time had never dragged like this before.

But...Now she had a good reason to give Johnny a call.

She flipped to the back of her date book and quickly dialed the number he'd given her. The phone rang six times before it was picked up.

The man who answered had a heavy French accent, and Chelsea didn't catch the restaurant's name. It might have been Lou's or Louie's, but she wasn't sure.

"Is John Anziano there, please?" she asked.

"Who this is?"

"Chelsea Spencer."

"Who?"

She tried to speak slowly and clearly. "Chelsea."

"You say you call from Chelsea?" Chelsea was also the name of one of the towns north of Boston.

"No, Chelsea's my *name*," she tried to explain.

"*Oui, is what I asking you. For your name?*"

"*Please,*" Chelsea said, giving up. "Just tell Johnny his wife is on the phone."

"Aha! Hold now."

It was nearly a full minute before the line was picked up, and Johnny said, "My *wife*'s on the phone." He laughed. "Sorry it took me so long, but I'm not used to having a wife, and I was sure Jean-Paul had made a mistake, and that the phone was for Jim or Philippe, who *do* have wives. Jean-Paul's English is a little basic."

"So of course he's the one who answers the

phone," Chelsea said, happy beyond belief to hear his familiar, husky voice.

"He's the dessert chef. He just happened to be the only one of us not up to his elbows in lobster bisque. So what's up?"

*I'm drowning in an ocean of debt and despair and I wanted to hear your voice.* "Actually, I'm calling because I was hoping it would be okay if we changed tonight's plans a little bit."

He was silent for a moment, and when he spoke she could tell he'd stopped smiling. "Change them, huh? You mean, cancel them?"

*No!* she nearly shouted into the phone before she caught herself. "God, no. I was just wondering if you'd mind if I came to your place instead."

"No, but... Are you sure that's what you want to do?" He lowered his voice. "I was looking forward to using that key you gave me."

Chelsea swallowed. "I was too. But I put the condo on the market this afternoon, and there's going to be about two dozen realtors walking through the place at seven-thirty tomorrow morning."

"You're selling your condo?"

"I have to," she told him. "I still have those loan

payments to make. As it is, even if I sell the thing tomorrow, I'm going to be late with the first payment."

"So...are you going to...Do you...intend to move in to my place? With me?"

His voice sounded funny, and Chelsea was instantly anxious. "Not if you don't want me to. I guess I thought, since we're going to be married for a whole year..."

"Are you kidding? Where else would you live? It would be weird if you lived anywhere else. I mean, you're my wife, right?" He laughed. "I know because Jean-Paul said so, and he's French, and everyone knows the French know everything. I just thought you'd probably want us to live at your place."

"No, I've got to sell it," Chelsea said. "I need the cash, and besides, it's too far away from the office anyway. I've actually been thinking about selling for a while."

He snorted. "What a liar. You told me you just finished renovating the bathroom."

"Well, it turns out I don't really like the color tile I chose for the floor, so—" She broke off, realizing she wasn't fooling him—or herself. "It sucks.

But the alternative is to borrow money from my father, and the fact is, I'd rather try to sell my condo first."

"Because you think asking your dad for money will be admitting you failed."

"Are you going to tell me where you live, or will I have to track down your address through the phone company?"

"You're changing the subject," he noted.

"Give the man a cigar. Come on, I've got my pen ready. Stop psychoanalyzing me and tell me how to get to your place."

She quickly wrote down the directions Johnny gave her.

"Look, I've got to get back to work," he told her then. "I'm trying to speed things along so I can get out of here at a reasonable hour. The way it looks right now, I'll definitely be able to leave by ten."

"So... I guess I'll see you at, say, ten-oh-one...?"

Johnny laughed. "How about ten-thirty? I'll want to take a shower right away and maybe vacuum the living-room rug."

"You don't have to do that."

"Yeah, well, it's not every day that your wife

comes over to your condo for the first time. First impressions count, you know."

Chelsea laughed.

"No rude comments about silly T-shirts, please," Johnny continued. "Look, I've got to run. You know I'd love to talk to you more...."

"Go," Chelsea told him. "And call me if you think you'll be done sooner."

"Oh, I will." He paused, and when he spoke again his voice was huskier than usual. "I'll see you later."

"Bye, John." Chelsea hung up the phone and looked at her watch: 2:30. Eight more hours. She rolled her eyes in exasperation.

God, would this day *never* end?

There was a pair of boxer shorts hanging from the back of one of Johnny's dining-room chairs. He scooped it up as he breezed past on his way up-stairs, taking off his shirt and kicking off his shoes and pants as he went.

He took the quickest shower in the history of Western civilization and vacuumed the living-room rug as he dried himself off.

He slipped into a clean pair of jeans and a plain red T-shirt, and then quickly set the table.

He'd turned on the oven the moment he came through the door, and it was preheated enough now to put in the still-warm containers of food he'd brought home from the restaurant.

He'd made a lamb stew early in the afternoon, and it had simmered all day, along with his buzzing anticipation, constantly reminding him of the night to come. Now the meat was so tender it seemed to melt from the pressure of a fork.

The sauce was up to his usual near-perfection standards, delicate and light, with a flavor that added to the richness of the lamb rather than covering it up. This was going to be a five-star meal. He couldn't wait to see Chelsea's face as she tasted it. He couldn't wait to watch her eyes as she realized the man she'd married was well on his way to becoming a master chef. He knew she hadn't asked him about his work because she'd been embarrassed for him—working in a restaurant. She probably thought he was a glorified waiter or a sous chef at best.

The water he'd put into a pot when he'd first come in finally reached a rolling boil, and he quickly rinsed a cupful of basmati rice and tossed it in with a dash of salt and a pat of butter. He stirred once, then put the lid on and turned down the heat. The rice's fragrant aroma soon filled the house.

He'd brought fresh lettuce and vegetables already cut for a salad from the restaurant, and he tossed them together in a cut-glass bowl and placed it on the table along with a small bottle of his own apple-cider vinaigrette dressing.

As he lit the candle in the center of the table, the doorbell chimed. Hoping he hadn't missed picking up any of the stray laundry that magically seemed to appear around the house, he went to open the door.

He took a deep breath before he pulled it open, but still, the sight of Chelsea standing on the steps outside nearly knocked him over.

His wife. Her blond hair was loose around her shoulders, and underneath her jacket she was dressed as he was, in jeans and a T-shirt, a gold wedding band around her left ring finger, and a matching blaze of desire in her eyes.

"Honey, I'm home," she said, in a decent enough imitation of Ricky Ricardo.

He laughed, but then stopped, afraid he sounded as giddy as he felt. He opened the door wider to let her in. "Did you have any trouble parking?" he asked, trying to sound casual, knowing that grabbing her and pulling her inside, tossing her over one shoulder in a fireman's hold and carrying her up to his bedroom to tear off her clothes and bury himself inside of her would not be good form.

"No," she told him. "I took a cab."

Neither would pinning her to the wall with a soul-shattering kiss as his fingers found the zipper of her jeans and...

She was carrying a leather gym bag over one shoulder, and he took it from her as he closed the door behind her. His fingers brushed the warmth of her shoulder as an intimate whiff of her sweet perfume invaded his senses. He had to close his eyes briefly in an attempt to steady himself.

He watched her glance around the small entryway, taking in his somewhat eccentric collection of mismatched watercolors on the walls, and the soft—and recently vacuumed—beige carpeting underneath her feet. She looked at the stairs going up to the bedrooms, at the old-fashioned coatrack and umbrella stand in the corner, and the rather battered antique that served as a table for the telephone.

She stood back, slightly ill at ease, waiting for him to lead the way. This was going to be her home for the next year, but right now she was a guest here. "Something smells great."

"Yeah. I thought we could have a late dinner. Did you eat?"

For a moment she looked a little odd. "No," she said. "But I'm not very hungry—I haven't had much of an appetite lately, and..."

He set her bag down by the stairs and walked backward into the great room, unable to turn away from her for even a moment.

Chelsea looked astonished, then confused as she took in the huge single room that served as living area, dining room, and kitchen combined.

"This is beautiful," she murmured, looking at the vaulted ceiling, the sliders that led out to the deck that had a million-dollar view of the harbor, and the sparsely furnished yet comfortable-looking living area. She turned to look at him, narrowing her eyes accusingly. "You have money."

"Not really," he said, moving into the kitchen

and checking the rice. "Not the way your family has money."

"But this place must've cost—"

"It was bequeathed to my mother by one of her patients."

"I thought you told me she had a clinic near the Projects. How could one of her patients...?"

"His name was David Hauser," he told her. "He was about a million years old. He lived next door—we had no idea he owned prime real estate all over town—and my mother always made a point to stop in and see him after she came home, no matter how tired she was."

Johnny took a pair of wineglasses down from the cabinet as Chelsea perched atop one of the bar stools on the other side of the counter that separated the kitchen area from the rest of the room. She was watching him, her eyes following him as he moved around the kitchen.

"She always made me cook a little extra at dinner," he continued, "and take a plate over to Mr. H, even on the days we were stretched a little thin for cash. Sometimes, if I knew she was going to be really late, I'd take my plate over, too, and eat with him. He was very cool. He was born in 1875, so he could tell the most incredible stories about Boston, before the advent of the automobile. He'd lived through the turn of the century and both world wars. He was amazing. My mother was convinced he was going to live forever—and he damn near outlived her."

He took a deep breath. "After my mother was gone, I thought about selling, but I'd lived here with her the last year before she died, and I liked it here too much, you know? There's a little bit of Davey and my mom still here. Their spirits linger—and I don't mean in a bad way," he added hastily.

"I know what you mean," she murmured, resting her chin in the palm of her hand, still watching him with those impossibly blue eyes.

"I never had a place like this before," he told her, losing himself in the ocean of her eyes. "I always lived in crappy little basement apartments or fifth-floor walk-ups with a courtyard view of the neighbor's bathroom window. So I decided to stay and see what it was like to have a real home. That's when I put in this kitchen and did the rest of the renovations—I tore down the walls and opened this area up."

"Your mother and Davey would've approved," she told him. "It's gorgeous."

*She* was gorgeous, with the overhead light from the kitchen glinting off her golden hair as she turned to look out at the dimly lit dining area, the living space beyond that, and the harbor lights twinkling on the other side of the sliding glass doors. Even dressed down in jeans and a T-shirt, she looked glamorous.

"How about a glass of wine with dinner?" His voice sounded raspy, and he cleared his throat.

She turned to look at him. "Dinner?"

"Yeah. The rice is just about ready. What do you say we eat?"

She looked uneasy. "John, I realized when I walked in here that there's something kind of important about myself that I haven't told you. I mean, I didn't *think* to tell you, and it hasn't come up when we've talked, which is odd, because it usually does, but..."

Chelsea took a deep breath. "I'm a vegetarian."

As she watched, her words sunk in. Johnny first laughed at the absurdity, then gazed at her with questioning disbelief, then looked incredibly disappointed. Finally he tried to hide his disappointment with a smile.

"Well, damn," he said. "If I'd known, I'd have made something with chicken or fish."

She shook her head at his common mistake. "I'm a *vegetarian*. I don't eat chicken *or* fish. I follow the face rule."

"The what?"

"The face rule: If it used to have a face, I don't eat it. I also don't eat any milk or dairy, although I will eat eggs if they're cooked into a bread or a cake—John, I'm so sorry. You went to all this trouble to make this nice dinner...."

He definitely didn't look happy. "So what *do* you eat?"

"Lots of things. Beans, salad, pasta, tofu, vegetables—*lots* of vegetables...Just not meat of any kind."

"I'm not a vegetarian," he told her. "Obviously. Is it going to bother you to have meat around the house?"

"Not if you keep it in the kitchen."

He forced a smile as he crossed the kitchen and turned off both the oven and the burner under the pot of rice on the stove and made his own attempt at humor. "At least I found out before our appearance on *The Newlywed Game*. We would have lost big points, me not knowing this one."

"There's still so much we don't know about each other," Chelsea mused. "Yet here we are, about to live together as if we're really married for a whole year."

She found herself watching the loose-fitting cut of his jeans and the more snug fit of his T-shirt, the red cotton hugging his muscular chest and shoulders. His hair was still damp from his shower, combed back from his face and curling around his neck. He looked unbearably delicious.

"We *are* really married," he said quietly.

She looked up and into the midnight brown of his eyes, and the entire world seemed to tilt around her. He was right. They *were* really married, with rings and a marriage license and everything. And in just a few minutes—if she could make her rubbery legs work well enough to climb down off this stool—they were going to go upstairs together and consummate that marriage.

He turned and took a bottle of white wine from the refrigerator, and poured some into one of the glasses. He paused and looked up at her, bottle poised, ready to fill the second. She couldn't begin to interpret the look in his eyes. "Do you drink wine?"

"Not usually. No. It's not...I...No, I don't."

He nodded, setting the bottle down beside the empty glass as he took a generous sip from the other, swirling the wine around his mouth before he swallowed.

"I'm sorry," she said again.

He looked at her. "*I'm* the one who should be apologizing. It never even occurred to me to ask if you were a vegetarian." He forced another smile. "I guess we could send out for pizza—" He swore sharply. "Except you don't eat cheese, right?"

Chelsea slid off her stool and moved toward the end of the counter. "I'm not hungry right now. I'd rather see the rest of your condo anyway. What's upstairs?"

Johnny looked at her, standing there, leaning slightly against the edge of his kitchen counter. She knew damn well what was upstairs. The bedrooms. His bedroom. His bed.

Heaven. Heaven was upstairs.

She smiled at him, a smile that was bewitchingly sexy, and he instantly released his disappointment.

Just like that, it was filed away, to be worked through at a later time. She was a vegetarian, and he was well on his way to becoming a master chef, specializing in dishes made with veal and lamb. By choice, his own wife would never taste his most magnificent creations. Of course, she would only be his wife for one year. But he refused to think about any of that now.

She held out her hand to him. "Will you show me the rest of your condo?"

She wanted to go upstairs.

He may have totally blown the chance for a romantic dinner through his ignorance, but there was no way he could possibly blow this. He'd wanted her for far too long.

Still, he couldn't seem to do more than whisper, "I'd love to." Her fingers were cool as he took her hand and led her back down the hallway. As they passed he grabbed her gym bag with his free hand and carried it with them up the stairs.

He tried to stop at the first door off the upstairs hallway. "This is my home office."

But Chelsea only glanced in. "Which one's your bedroom?"

"The door on the left."

She slipped free from his grasp, and pausing only to glance back at him with another of those incredible smiles, she disappeared into the darkness of his room.

He followed her in, setting her bag down near the door.

The curtains were open, revealing more sliders like the ones downstairs and a similar view of the harbor. The moonlight streaming in gave the room a ghostly glow, and Johnny didn't switch on the overhead light.

He watched her make her way around the big room. His closet door was open, and as she passed she fingered one of the shirts hanging there. She trailed her hand along the polished wood of his dresser, along the huge bookshelf that lurked against one wall, along the metal frame of the NordicTrack system he had set up with other exercise gear in the corner of the room, working her way around to his bed.

She turned to face him then, across the wide expanse of his bedspread. "I was thinking that right about now would be a really good time for you to kiss me."

He took his time walking around the bed, each

step filled with the pleasure of his anticipation. She met him halfway, impatient with his pace, and kissed him, instead.

Her lips were so soft, her entire body melting into his. Johnny laughed aloud and heard her join in.

"This is going to be really good, isn't it?" she whispered, looking searchingly into his eyes.

He could feel her heart pounding, feel his beating an answering tattoo. "Oh, yeah." He kissed her again, harder this time. This was going to be beyond good.

He felt her hands sliding up underneath the edge of his T-shirt, her palms gliding along his bare back, and he knew, despite his intentions to make love to Chelsea slowly, he couldn't wait a second longer.

He tugged at her shirt, pulling it free from the waistband of her jeans, filling his hands with the soft weight of her breasts as she fell back with him onto the bed.

Her legs were around him, and she kissed him fiercely. She tugged at his T-shirt, and he helped her pull it over his head, then did the same with her shirt. His fingers fumbled with the front clasp of her bra, and she quickly unfastened it for him.

He pulled back then, wanting to look at her, wanting to see her desire for him in the tautness of her nipples and the swell of her perfect breasts, in the way she lay there on his bed, half-naked and waiting for him, in the heat in her eyes.

"Touch me," she whispered, and he did. With his hands, with his mouth. He buried his face in her incredible softness.

He could feel her unfastening her jeans, and he helped her pull them off. Her legs were long and smooth and gracefully shaped and he laughed again because he couldn't believe he was actually running his hands along them.

Chelsea smiled at Johnny's laughter as he slid her panties down her legs.

She pulled him down on top of her, and before he kissed her, he gazed into her eyes and gave her a heart-stoppingly gorgeous smile. "I'm overcome by the need to spout a cliché," he told her.

"Such as?" Chelsea's heart kicked into overdrive. Was he going to tell her that he was falling in love with her?

He gave her a kiss that rocked her as he ran one hand up her leg, all the way up her thigh and even farther. He touched her, gently at first, slowly, softly, and all coherent thought vanished from her mind. She found herself reaching for the button of his jeans, wanting to feel his skin against hers.

"Such as, you're so incredibly beautiful, just looking at you makes me dizzy," he murmured, trailing kisses from her mouth down to her breasts.

He didn't mention whether or not he loved her and Chelsea didn't know whether to feel relieved or disappointed. And then she didn't feel anything but desire as he shifted his weight to allow her better access to the zipper of his jeans, as still he touched her, stroked her, harder now, deeper.

It was her turn to laugh aloud as she wrestled the zipper down and discovered he was wearing no underwear—just the way she'd described that night on the phone. And, as she'd also described, his arousal gave her powerful proof of his desire. He was totally, incredibly male.

She looked up into his eyes and he caught his breath as she touched him.

As she gazed at him something seemed to explode, and the passion they had kept buried between them for so long fireballed. He kissed her almost savagely, possessively, and she kissed him back just as ferociously. She'd never felt anything so intense ever before, and it terrified her, bringing tears to her eyes, but she couldn't have stopped had her life depended on it.

His hands were everywhere, touching, stroking, driving her wild with need. He paused only to cover himself and protect them both, and then he was on top of her, between her legs, and she was lifting herself up, seeking him, wanting him, needing to feel him, *all* of him, inside her, possessing her.

Owning her, body as well as heart and soul. No, *no*. She couldn't think that way. She *wouldn't* think that way....

"Look at me," he whispered. "Chelsea, open your eyes."

She did, looking up into his beautiful, familiar, lovely eyes. He watched her face as he filled her, his satisfaction evident in the hot, fierce smile he gave her. "Now you're *really* my wife," he said.

For a year. Only for a year. She pressed her hips up, pushing him deeply inside of her, in an attempt to show him that she was still in control. But she was the one who cried out.

And when he began to move, setting a rhythm that made her heart pound, she knew that when it came to Johnny, she hadn't truly been in control since the morning she asked him to marry her. Ever since that moment she'd been careening down a hill toward a cliff, in danger of falling crazily in love with this man, destined to crash, her life as she knew it shattered into a million irreparable tiny pieces.

But as she went over the edge, as her heart as well as her body was engulfed in waves of sheer, tempestuous, exquisite pleasure, she found a pure, uninhibited freedom in her lack of control. The fall would probably kill her, but dear God, all she was feeling was well worth it.

She felt Johnny's release, heard him cry out her name again and again, his voice like velvet, both smooth and rough against her sensitized skin, as he drove himself deeply inside of her one final, delicious time.

She heard him sigh, a deep exhale thick with satisfaction, and she closed her eyes, waiting to fall like a stone back to earth, preparing for the shock of impact.

But Johnny's arms were around her, holding her, keeping her safe. And she realized she wasn't going to crash.

At least not for a year.

# TWELVE

———

THE PHONE RANG as the first streaks of dawn were lighting the sky outside the bedroom windows.

Chelsea felt Johnny reach for the receiver. " 'lo?" He spoke softly, trying not to wake her. She heard him swear softly. "Did you try calling Carlos?" Another pause. "Yeah, I figured you did, but . . . How about Bobby?"

With his hair rumpled, his eyes sleepier than usual, and a night's growth of beard on his face, he looked impossibly sexy. He looked like someone she would wake up next to in bed only in her wildest dreams.

"It's me or no one, huh? Can you get the truck loaded for me?" He sighed and ran his hand through his hair. "Look, Doreen, I know you've got stuff to do in the office, but last night was my wedding night, and my bride's not going to appreciate me deserting her this morning for any longer than I absolutely have to, and—Yes, I said bride." He laughed softly. "Yeah, I'm married. Wild, huh? She's incredible, and I'm going to be in a big hurry to get back to her, so if you guys in the office can at least load the truck—"

Chelsea shifted, stretching her legs, and he turned to look at her, an apology in his eyes. "I'm sorry, I was trying not to wake you." He spoke into the phone. "Hold on a second, Doreen."

He covered the receiver, leaned forward, and kissed Chelsea on the mouth. "Good morning."

She smiled at him, snuggling closer and sliding her leg across his. "Rumor has it I'm incredible."

"Oh, yeah." He kissed her again, longer this time, and she could feel his body's instant response. "It's no rumor—it's the cold, hard truth. You're totally off the scale."

"Do you often get phone calls from women at dawn?"

He grinned. "Only from women named Doreen, who work at Meals on Wheels."

She ran her fingers lightly across his chest, delighting in the feel of his muscles and the soft, springy hair that covered them. "She wants to take you away from me, huh?"

"Just for a couple hours. I'll be back before you know it."

"Do you really have to go?" She let her hand drift lower, and he closed his eyes.

"If I don't, some of these people won't eat for a day." He opened his eyes and smiled at her. "But I sure as hell can be late." He brought the phone back to his ear. "Doreen? I'll be there. In forty-five minutes." He laughed. "I *know* it usually takes me ten minutes to get over there, but today it's going to take me forty-five, *capisce*?"

As he reached to hang up the phone Chelsea straddled him and lightly ran her cheek against his morning beard as she kissed her way to his mouth. "Since I'm the one who's making you late, maybe I should come along and help you with your deliveries."

He lifted her chin with one hand and looked searchingly into her eyes. "Really?"

"I'd like to—if it's all right with you..."

There was a softness in Johnny's eyes as he gazed up at her. "You *are* incredible."

Chelsea shook her head. "No, I'm not. *You* are. *You* want to make sure the people on that route get their food today. *My* motives are purely selfish. I want to get you back here, in bed, as soon as I can."

He kissed her and she closed her eyes, aware that she had nearly revealed too much. She'd nearly told him the real reason she wanted to make his deliveries with him. She'd nearly admitted that she wanted simply to be with him. It was better to let him think her reasons were based on sex rather than some deep emotion she couldn't even begin to identify—some deep emotion she *refused* to identify. And it would be better for *her* if she kept her straying emotions securely out of Johnny's reach and firmly in control.

She kissed him again, closing her eyes, knowing that when it came to Johnny, her control was in short supply.

"You're late."

Johnny turned to look at Chelsea and smiled. "I

know, Mr. Gruber. But Evan got sick, and I was called in to drive the truck at the last minute. I got here as soon as I could."

They'd made over a dozen stops, and almost every person they'd brought food to had informed Johnny that he was late. And every time they told him that, he'd looked at Chelsea and smiled, and she knew he was remembering, in detail, exactly *why* he'd been late.

She could hardly wait to go back home and make him late for his work at the restaurant too.

The old man squinted at Chelsea. "You training a new girl?"

"No, sir," Johnny told him. "This is Chelsea. My wife." He still laughed whenever he said that. "I brought her over here to meet you."

Chelsea shook Mr. Gruber's hand. At one time he'd been remarkably tall, but time had made him stooped and thin, and now he was a narrow tower of a man. His hair was pure white and it grew thick and full. The thick lenses of his glasses made his eyes seem huge in his wrinkled face, but they were still a vivid shade of blue.

"I'm pleased to meet you," she said.

"Pretty girl," the elderly man told Johnny, shuffling into the kitchen, leaning heavily on a thick, wooden cane. "Your wife, huh? How'd you manage that one?" He laughed, a dry wheezing cackle.

"Wow, you're really a laugh riot today, Mr. G," Johnny said good-naturedly as he put a wrapped sandwich and a plate of microwave-ready food into the refrigerator.

"No, no, I'm just teasing, just teasing. Can't think of anyone more deserving of such a pretty girl's love." He turned to Chelsea and shook one finger at her. "You take good care of my friend Johnny."

"I will."

My friend Johnny. At every delivery stop, there had been someone—someone elderly or someone ill—that Johnny had made smile with his cheerful banter and friendly jokes. It was clear to Chelsea that he brought them far more than nourishing food.

He brought color into the grayness of their lives—the same way he'd splashed a psychedelic swirl of emotions and sensations onto the monochromatic sameness of her own life.

"What've we got for breakfast today?" Mr. Gruber asked Johnny.

"Standard fare, Mr. G. Cornflakes, bran flakes, crisp rice, or—drumroll please—instant oatmeal!"

"I think I've got some fresh eggs in the icebox. If I ask very nicely, might you scramble me a pair of eggs?"

Johnny laughed. "You know I will, Mr. G, but you also know as well as I do that what you really want is a bowl of instant oatmeal with brown sugar on top."

"Come to think of it, you're right," the old man mused. He grinned at Chelsea. "I've got a bit of a sweet tooth."

"You have an entire mouthful of sweet teeth, old man," Johnny teased, setting about making the oatmeal.

"At my age, it's a wonder I have any teeth at all!"

"At *your* age? What, do you really think eighty-four years is some kind of accomplishment or something, Mr. G? You want to boast about your age, you should wait until you hit a really big number, like one hundred. Then you can say things like 'at *my* age.'"

Chelsea smiled, recognizing that this conversation was one the two men had probably had every time Johnny came to visit.

"Do you know, Chelsea works just a few blocks away from here, Mr. G," Johnny said.

"Oh," the old man said darkly as he sat down to eat his bowl of oatmeal. "That's not good." He turned to look at Chelsea. "This neighborhood isn't what it used to be. I've lived here thirty years—no, forty years now—and I don't go out at night anymore. It's not safe."

"Fifty-four years," Johnny reminded him. "You moved in right after World War Two, remember? You were just out of the service."

"That's right. Martin was just a baby, and—" He broke off, a look of confusion crossing his face. "I don't know why he won't write. I told him to write when he's away at camp...."

"How's the oatmeal, Mr. G? Did I put enough brown sugar on, or do you want to add a little more?"

"This is delightful, thank you."

The old man ate quietly, suddenly subdued. Whoever Martin was, he deserved to be strung up for not writing or visiting.

Johnny kept up a steady stream of conversation as he made short work of a pile of dirty dishes in the sink. But nothing he said seemed to bring Mr. Gruber out of his introspective mood.

"Ready for a quick game of cards?" Johnny asked, when Mr. Gruber had scraped his bowl clean.

Mr. Gruber carefully set his spoon down next to the empty bowl. "Not today, I don't think. I'm a bit tired. If you don't mind, I'll head in for a nap."

In the course of the past few minutes the old man had seemed to age a dozen years.

"How about I give you a hand into the other room?" Johnny asked quietly.

"Thank you."

As Chelsea watched, the older man let Johnny help him out of his chair, and together, they walked slowly down the hall to the bedroom.

"I'll give you a call later to remind you to put that dinner in the microwave," she heard Johnny tell Mr. G.

"All right, Martin."

"Should I pull down the shades or do you want to be able to look out the window? I know you like to watch the clouds. . . ."

"Leave them up, thank you."

"Okay, I'll see you later—probably not for another few days, so be nice to Bobby or Carlos or whoever comes out here. No fair trying to win their paychecks with your card games."

"All right, Martin."

"It's Johnny, Mr. G," Johnny said softly. "Johnny Anziano from Meals on Wheels. Remember?"

Johnny headed down the hall toward Chelsea, and she could hear the old man's voice, quavering now, calling after him, "Martin, call me if you're going to be late...."

Johnny briefly closed his eyes and shook his head very slightly. "It's Johnny," he called back. "And I *will* call you later."

Chelsea followed Johnny out the door and waited while he carefully locked both bolts. He stood there for a moment, just staring at his keys, and when he finally glanced over at her, he looked impossibly sad.

"He seemed like he was having a good day, but..."

"Why won't Martin visit?" she asked softly.

"Because he died when he was fourteen years old." Johnny sighed, shaking his head slightly. "I can do everything for Al Gruber but the one thing he truly wants. I can't be Martin."

Chelsea knew at that moment, as she gazed into brown eyes made even darker with compassion, that she had been fooling herself for days now. She knew with a certainty that rocked her to the core that despite her pretending otherwise, she had fallen desperately in love with her husband.

"Johnny, will you kiss me?" she whispered.

He smiled then. It was a small smile, but it was real. "Always," he murmured, pulling her into his arms.

He tasted like coffee sweetened with sugar and cream. He was both gentle and demanding, both sweet and full of passion, both powerful and yielding. He was smart and funny and kind and sexy. She loved the sound of his voice, the husky catch to it when he was turned on. She loved the way his smile could light up an entire room. She loved the way he watched her when she talked, the way he listened to her so intently, every cell in his body alert as if what she had to say truly mattered. She loved the way the laughter in his eyes could dissolve into instant, searing heat. She loved everything about him.

She loved him.

"Come on, let's get out of here," Johnny breathed into her ear. "I have to be at work in a couple of hours."

Holding his hand, Chelsea let him lead her down the four flights of stairs and out to where the Meals on Wheels truck was illegally parked in a loading zone.

"I've been thinking about what Mr. Gruber was saying," he told her as he unlocked the truck. "About this part of town being dangerous at night." He helped her up into the passenger seat, then crossed around in front of the truck.

Chelsea reached over and unlocked his door.

"Thanks," he said, climbing in. "So I was thinking, if you ever want to work late, you know, past dark, maybe you could call me at the restaurant, and I could pick you up on my way home."

"I work late almost every night," she told him.

"Then I'll meet you over there almost every night," he told her as he pulled out into the traffic.

"You don't have to do that." She didn't *want* him to do that.

"Yeah, I know—but I want to."

"It's out of your way."

"It'll take me an extra ten minutes. Big deal. Your safety's worth that to me."

"If it's late, I call a cab, and wait to unlock the door until I can see it out the front window," Chelsea said coolly. She was a grown woman, and she could take care of herself.

He glanced at her and laughed. "Uh-oh, I've conjured up the Ice Princess. I'm in trouble now."

"That's the second time you've called me that," Chelsea told him, exasperation tingeing her voice.

"I'm just teasing," he said. "You sometimes get a certain tone in your voice, and you start shooting icicles out of your eyes. It's just really different from the way you are the rest of the time, it's kind of funny, that's all."

Icicles from her eyes...She'd always thought that her father had had what she called "Siberian eyes." At times colder than cold. Was it possible that she did the same thing? "God, do I do it a lot?"

"No. Just when you're mad. Or scared—you know, when you're feeling threatened." He glanced at her again. "Like right now."

Chelsea nodded. "I don't want you to pick me up every night after work, as if I'm a child that needs to be taken care of. I don't want that kind of relationship."

"I've noticed your resistance to the idea," he said dryly. He pulled up to a red light and turned to look at her appraisingly. "Promise me you'll do the thing with the cab?"

She looked back at him. "I promise you that I'm smart enough and old enough and experienced enough to take care of myself."

"That's not quite the promise I wanted, but I guess it'll do," he said with a smile.

Chelsea found herself smiling back at Johnny, marveling at the way he'd taken a potentially volatile situation and defused it. Of course, the fact that he'd backed down had surely helped. If he had insisted on picking her up and driving her home every night, there would have been figurative bloodshed.

But he respected her enough to recognize that she *could* take care of herself. And he seemed to know that when it came to protecting her independence, she would not negotiate.

Chelsea watched the morning sunlight reflecting off his face, accentuating his rugged features, making his dark hair gleam. On the other hand, maybe she *would* negotiate. In fact, it was entirely likely that if she wasn't careful, she would find herself giving in.

Because she loved him that much.

She was hit with a wave of panic, and she tried to calm herself, taking a deep breath and letting it slowly out. It could be worse. She could very well be in love with a man who insisted on imposing his rules upon her.

But she was lucky—Johnny wasn't like that. And maybe, just maybe, he was the one man she could live with as equal partners, both giving and sharing. Maybe, she could stay strong and refuse to let herself love him so much that she would give up her self and her dreams just to be near him. And maybe—and she knew that she was asking for an awful lot of miracles here—if she were really lucky, over the course of the next year he'd come to love her too.

"Can we go home now?" she whispered.

Johnny smiled, and he put the truck in high gear.

It was after seven before Johnny could get away from the stove and give Chelsea a call. It was time for a break, and he took a cup of coffee into his office, closing the door behind him. There was a stack of papers that needed his signature in his in-basket, and as he dialed the phone he set to work skimming them quickly then signing his name.

He tried Chelsea's number at work, assuming since she went in late, she'd be there still, working late.

He was right—she picked up on the first ring. He paused in his signing, afraid the sound of her voice would make his hand shake.

"Spencer/O'Brien," she said shortly. She sounded overworked and overstressed and not very friendly.

"Hi, it's me. Is this a bad time to talk? I can call you later if you want...."

"John. Hi." Her voice warmed up considerably. "No, it's no better or worse than any other time. God, I'm glad you called."

Johnny took a sip of his coffee, feeling the jolt of the caffeine mingling jazzily with the electric feeling he got just from talking to Chelsea on the phone. Talking to his *wife* on the phone. She was his *wife*. He laughed aloud in pleasure at the bizarre thought. "I was wondering if you had plans for later. I figured since we only had lunch at three, you wouldn't have eaten yet."

"Are you asking me to dinner?"

The next stack of letters were form letters to their food suppliers, and he could sign them one after another without having to read each one through.

"You bet," he told her. "Do you think you can catch a cab over to the restaurant in a few hours? I promise I won't make you eat anything that ever had a face."

Chelsea laughed then lowered her voice. "I'd rather meet you at home. Right now."

Home. This wasn't the first time she'd referred to his condo as "home." Johnny felt a rush of happiness. His condo was their *home*. And she wanted to meet him there. Now. It seemed almost too good to be true. "I can't get away right now, but you know I would if I could."

"Are you absolutely sure you can't just sneak off? I've had a truly awful afternoon, and..." She sighed, and when she continued, her voice suddenly sounded so sad. "All I want is for you to hold me."

Johnny's heart lurched. "Chelsea, if I worked

for myself, I'd be at your office in an instant, but I don't. I work for a really nice guy named Rudy, who would be very unhappy if I left in the middle of the dinner rush." He glanced at the clock on his desk. As it was, he had to get back to the kitchen pretty soon. "Did something happen at work?"

She drew in a deep breath. "My father called. He didn't say anything directly, but it was a little obvious that he's waiting for me to come crawling, asking for money to pay back that bank loan."

He signed another letter. "Maybe he called because he thought by initiating a conversation, he might make it easier for you to ask him for the money."

She sighed again. "Well, whatever his motivation, I couldn't do it. Not over the phone. If I'm going to beg, at least I'm going to hang on to some shred of my pride by doing it in person. My parents are having some sort of party Sunday afternoon. I thought it would be a good time to corner my dad and grovel. I can get it over with, and he'll have all his party guests to distract him afterward, so I won't have to spend an hour or two listening to him lecture me on poor business decisions. I know it's your day off, and if you want, I can make up some kind of excuse for why you can't—"

Johnny put down his pen. "Don't be ridiculous. I want to go with you. I'd love to go with you."

She drew in an unsteady breath. "You're so sweet."

"I *insist* that I go with you—that is, unless you absolutely don't want me there?"

Her voice broke slightly. "I do want you there. Badly."

"Then I'm there."

"I think I'm going to cry. Say something to make me laugh, will you?"

"If you want to know the truth, I'm not sweet at all. The real reason I'm dying to go to this shindig is because I want to live out a certain fantasy I have of getting it on with you in your parents' guest bathroom—with a high-class party in full swing on the other side of the door."

Chelsea laughed breathlessly. "Oh, my God. That did it. Thank you."

"I'm serious."

"No, you're not."

"Wait until Sunday. You'll see." Johnny finished signing the last of the ordering invoices, and with unerring aim tossed the pen back into the coffee mug that held a variety of pencils and pens. "You know what? I need a picture of you for my desk. I'm sitting here, and I'm wishing desperately that I had a picture of you."

"You have a desk?" There was a trace of disbelief in her voice.

"I do. I have an office, too, with a door and everything. If you come over here, I'll show it to you. We can lock the door and live out my *other* fantasy about—"

"Very funny."

"This time I *am* kidding. Come on out here and have dinner with me, Chelsea. Please?"

"When do you want me over there? And where exactly is it?"

"Nine-thirty, quarter to ten." He quickly gave her the address.

"I'll be there."

"Take a cab."

"Right this way, madam."

Chelsea followed the maître d' through the hushed formal dining room at Lumière's.

Lumière's. Johnny worked at Lumière's. She remembered now that he'd told her that one of the first times they'd met. But she hadn't expected it, and therefore hadn't connected it to *this* Lumière's, which was, of course, *the* Lumière's on Beacon Street—Boston's premier gourmet restaurant.

She'd read a recent *Boston Globe* review of the restaurant, commending it on its ability to keep pace with the times and yet still consistently provide first-rate, four-star fare. They credited the restaurant's head chef and his young, capable staff—one of which surely was Johnny.

The stony-faced maître d' held open a door for her. "After you, madam."

"Thank you." There were plushly carpeted stairs on the other side of the door that led upward, and Chelsea climbed them. She turned back to glance at the maître d', who was now following her. "Where are we going?"

"To the private dining room, madam."

Lumière's fabled private dining room? Even Chelsea's father had never managed to get a reservation for Lumière's ultraexpensive, ultrachic private dining room.

It was a medium-sized room, decorated in tastefully muted colors, and only dimly lit by candles, both on the table and in candlesticks, scattered around the room. One wall was window, and it looked out over the street and the Boston Common below.

The table was set for two, with the simple elegance of a plain white linen cloth and shining black china. A bottle was chilling in a champagne bucket. Two tuxedo-clad waiters were standing attentively nearby, and at the maître d's nod, one of them picked up a telephone and discreetly dialed a number. The other held back a chair for her, then slipped the cloth napkin onto her lap.

"Mr. Anziano will be right with you, Mrs. Anziano." The maître d' bowed and quietly headed back down the stairs.

Mrs. Anziano. Funny, she kind of liked being called that. It was against all she believed in, as far as choosing to keep her own name despite being married, but it made her feel good.

Mrs. Anziano. It brought to mind images of a certain *Mister* Anziano lying next to her in bed, his heavily lidded eyes sleepy and warm as he held her after making love. It brought to mind images of him joining her in the shower, water streaming around them as they freely gave in to passion and desire. . . .

The waiters had resumed their soldierly stances near a door that no doubt led down a back staircase to the kitchen, and Chelsea smiled at them, hoping that neither was capable of mind reading. But they were like the guards to Buckingham Palace, and they didn't smile in return.

She smoothed down the skirt of her business suit, feeling much too underdressed for Lumière's. *Lumière's.* She still couldn't believe Johnny worked *here.* . . .

The door opened beside the waiters, and Johnny stepped into the room.

He was wearing a brown suit, and again, as on the day they'd met with the lawyer, his shirt and tie were shadings of the same color. Johnny smiled at her as he breezed toward the table, and before she could rise to her feet, he bent over and kissed her.

His hair was slightly damp and his cheeks were baby soft, as if he'd just shaved. He was wearing the slightest hint of a deliciously exotic-smelling cologne.

"Don't get up," he told her. He dragged the

chair around from the opposite side of the table so that he was sitting next to her rather than across from her. The waiters scurried instantly to move the plates and silverware and countless wineglasses around. "Are you hungry?"

She couldn't believe how good he looked. "Did you go home to shower and change? You should have told me you were going to do that."

"No, I didn't, actually. I keep a couple of suits here at work," he told her. He nodded to the waiters and they disappeared. "I take a quick shower and put one on just about every night before I come up to the private dining room."

Chelsea didn't understand. "Why do you come up here?"

"When people pay as much as they do to eat in Lumière's private dining room, they usually want to meet the chef."

"The chef?" She was stunned. "You mean the *main* chef? The chief chef? The four-star review in *The Boston Globe* chef?"

Johnny was laughing at her. "That's me. The head honcho, top of the pecking order, I-give-the-commands, don't-mess-with-my-special-sauce chef."

He was watching her, gauging her reaction. He'd

known full well that she hadn't thought he was anything more than one of the lowly kitchen staff. She judged him and made incorrect assumptions based on the way he looked and the neighborhood he'd grown up in. She was as narrow-minded as her father.

"God, you must think I'm a jerk," she whispered. "You told me you worked here, and I assumed the worst instead of the best."

He touched the side of her face, his eyes as gentle as his fingers. "Hey, come on. I didn't plan this dinner to make you feel bad. I thought you would think it was funny. When we met I was driving a truck and wearing jeans. It's natural you wouldn't have expected me to be the head chef of a gourmet restaurant."

"It's natural, but it's also close-minded. Johnny, I'm so sorry."

He kissed her. "Apology accepted. Now lighten up, okay?" She didn't answer, and he kissed her again. "Okay?"

Chelsea nodded, and he kissed her one more time. "Good."

Johnny turned toward the champagne bucket, and one of the waiters appeared instantly, holding the bottle out for him to see. Johnny took it from him, holding it in turn for Chelsea.

"Oh," she said, shaking her head, "I don't—" But then she saw the label. It was nonalcoholic. It was sparkling grape juice.

"Does it have your approval?" Johnny asked.

She nodded.

Johnny handed the bottle back to the waiter, who opened it and poured them both a glass.

Chelsea couldn't speak through the lump in her throat. He'd gone to a lot of trouble to get that bottle specially for her. And she suspected getting that bottle had been the least of his efforts. She suspected that she was in for the meal of a lifetime. She knew for dead certain she was in for the year of her lifetime.

Johnny lifted his glass. "What should we toast?"

She shook her head, hoping that he'd want to toast the new level of their relationship, hoping he'd say something, *anything* that would give her hope to believe that he loved her too.

"I know what we can toast." He lifted his glass even higher. "Here's to never having to ask your father for money ever again."

Chelsea groaned. "Please. I don't want to have to think about that right now."

"You don't have to think about it ever again," Johnny told her, clinking his glass against hers and taking a sip. He set his wineglass down and reached into the inside pocket of his jacket. He took out an envelope and handed it to Chelsea. "I think there's probably enough in there to cover the first six payments of your loan."

For the second time that evening Chelsea was stunned. She stared at him. Just stared at him. "What did you just say?" she finally breathed.

Johnny tapped the envelope. "There's a bank check in here," he said. "I wasn't sure I'd be able to get the money out—I had it in a long-term CD—so I didn't want to say anything to you until I talked to the bank officer. But I went over there this afternoon and the penalties weren't that high, so..." He shrugged and smiled. "You don't need to ask your father for anything."

Chelsea lifted the envelope's flap and peeked at the dollar amount written on the check. "This is your savings," she said softly, her eyes filling with tears as she looked back at him.

"Part of it."

"Why are you doing this?"

"Because you're my wife."

"I'm not *really* your wife, Johnny. Not *really*."

Johnny glanced up at the two waiters. "Can we have some privacy, please?" When the two men vanished, he looked back at Chelsea and took her hand. "We're married. From now until the day it's over we're really married. You're *really* my wife and you need this money. So, I'm giving it to you."

"But I thought..." She lowered her voice as if the walls might have ears. "I thought you were saving to open your own restaurant."

"Twenty-five percent of your grandfather's trust will more than pay me back," he told her, putting the situation in terms he knew she would understand. "In a year I'll have more than enough to open my own place." He smiled. "At the rate I was saving, that puts me about five years ahead of schedule. You're making my dreams come true. The least I can do is return the favor."

Chelsea gazed at him. Money. This was about money. For a moment she'd almost forgotten that their marriage was first and foremost a business deal. He was merely making a wise investment, using his savings to ensure her happiness, in turn ensuring that their sham of a marriage would survive an entire year, which would enable him to receive his share of her inheritance.

Silly her. She'd been sitting here hoping that he would gaze at her with those soulful brown eyes and tell her he was giving her this money because he loved her.

She took a deep breath and forced a smile. "Well, you're full of surprises tonight." She handed the envelope back to him. "I'd like it if you could hold on to this—at least until we get...back to your place." Home. Lately she'd caught herself calling Johnny's condo "home." She had to stop doing that, because it *wasn't* her home. It was merely her temporary residence until...How had Johnny put it? Until the day it was over. She had to remember that it *was* going to be over. And soon. A year would fly past more quickly than she could believe.

"I'll have my lawyer draw up a loan agreement," she added.

"That's not necessary."

"I'd prefer it," she told him.

He nodded. "As you wish."

Chelsea forced herself to stop wishing for things

she couldn't have. She forced herself to stop thinking about the money and the future. She was with
Johnny right now, and dammit, she was going to
enjoy every minute of it. "So . . . what's for dinner?"

Johnny smiled.

"You would not *believe* what this man was able to
do with a pile of vegetables, a chunk of tofu, and
some spices," Chelsea told Moira. She shook her
head, still disbelieving. "I've never tasted anything
like that dinner in my entire life. He's some kind of
culinary genius."

Moira was watching her, chin in her hand, eyebrow raised.

Chelsea had to look away. "I'm gushing, I
know. Isn't it awful?"

"Sounds to me like Johnny Anziano should
change his last name to Right—as in Mr. Right.
Gee, and he's already your husband. How conven-
ient."

"He's my husband for a year. *Only* for a year."

"So when the year end approaches you
renegotiate—"

"He's got plans." Chelsea hated the sound of

pure, aching despair in her voice. "He's going to use his share of the trust to open his own restaurant, but before he does that he wants to go to Paris, to study with some kind of famous master chef for three months." She rushed to explain before Moira could interrupt. "You see, after dinner, we went downstairs into the kitchen, and he showed me his office—Moira, he's got this huge, gorgeous office, and the walls are *covered* with newspaper and magazine reviews and awards— and I just happened to look on his desk and see this application that was half filled out for a special advanced cooking program in Paris being offered by the International Culinary Institute."

"You just *happened* to see it." Moira grinned. "And you being you, you couldn't just mind your own business."

Chelsea slumped over her desk, resting her forehead on her arms and closing her eyes, reliving the dread she'd felt when she'd spotted the word *Paris* on the application. "He lived with a woman for nearly three years, and she still lives in Paris. I couldn't *not* ask about that application."

"And he said?"

"He didn't mention Raquel, of course. But he

told me getting accepted to this program was the ultimate nod from the international gourmet community. Only seven chefs are accepted each year. He told me his chances of getting in are extremely slim, and he reassured me that if he did get in, he wouldn't leave for Paris until next May."

"So maybe by next May we'll be doing well enough with the business that you can take a three-month leave of absence and go to Paris with him."

"He didn't ask me if I wanted to go."

"Give the man a chance. He hasn't been accepted into the program yet."

"And what if the business needs me here?"

"Then you're going to have to make some choices. Chels, if you love this guy—"

"No," Chelsea said, trying hard to convince herself that her words were true. "I don't love him that much. I refuse to love anyone that much."

"There are a million options. We could hire someone to fill in for you temporarily—"

"Do you know what John's specialty is?"

Moira snickered. "I can guess, but then again, you probably don't mean *that*. You probably mean his specialty as a chef."

Chelsea threw a telephone notepad at her friend. "Of course I mean his specialty as a chef."

"No, I don't know. Why don't you tell me?"

"Veal and lamb. Baby cows and baby sheep. I will never eat the food that *The Boston Globe* describes as 'culinary heaven,' and 'edible art.' I *can't* eat it, Mo. I *won't* eat it. And just how long do you really think he's going to want me hanging around, *not* eating his specialty?" Chelsea put her head in her hands again. "And the really stupid thing is, I keep finding myself thinking, well, maybe I can be a vegetarian only part of the time. Maybe I could eat his veal dishes every now and then." She lifted her head and looked miserably at Moira. "I'm actually considering giving up being a vegetarian—something I truly, honestly believe in for health reasons and for humanitarian reasons—just to please some guy who's good in bed."

"Some guy who's good in bed, whom you happen to be in love with," Moira pointed out.

"What am I going to do?"

"Whatever you do, *definitely* don't tell *him* how you feel," Moira said sarcastically, then ducked to avoid being hit with more flying office supplies.

# THIRTEEN

CHELSEA'S FATHER DEFINITELY knew. Johnny had known from the look in his eyes when the man shook his hand, right when he and Chelsea had walked in the door of the stately Tudor-style house.

So it was no real surprise when Howard Spencer pulled him away from the other guests to ask, "So, who are you, really?"

"Giovanni Anziano," Johnny said. "My friends call me Johnny."

"And from where exactly did Chelsea dig you up?"

Johnny tried to smile pleasantly despite the rude tone of Mr. Spencer's voice. He could understand how a father might be a little bit upset to find out his daughter had married a man who was a complete stranger to her family. "Actually, we met as a result of Chelsea getting her purse snatched."

"Her purse..." Something flickered in Spencer's eyes. "She never told me about that."

"I'm sure most children don't tell their parents about a lot of things."

"And she met you when?"

"No, I wasn't the one who mugged her," Johnny said, his words only half-joking. "I got her purse back for her and helped her get cleaned up."

"So naturally, in gratitude, she married you."

Johnny laughed. "Hey, that's a good one, Mr. S."

"I wasn't joking."

Johnny gave up trying to play nice. He lowered his voice and stepped closer to the older man. "Look, the fact is, I'm married to your daughter. I *like* being married to your daughter, and I intend to treat her really well, so you don't have to—"

"The *fact* is," Howard Spencer interrupted, "Chelsea married you solely to acquire her inheritance. I applaud her ingenuity but question her choice of…business partners. I'm just warning you, in one year, when this farce of a marriage is over, you will take whatever deal she's made with you and quietly slink back to whatever hole you came out of. If you don't attempt to stay married to her, or to contest the divorce in *any* way, I'll triple whatever payment she gives you. And I'm prepared to make you that offer in writing."

Triple. Just like that, one truckload of money could become three. But what good would three truckloads of money be without Chelsea to share it with him?

"You know where to reach me when you decide to take the money," Mr. Spencer said with smug certainty, then walked away.

Johnny's heart was pounding and his mouth was dry. God, what he would have given to deck that guy. Just one punch, that's all he wanted. Of course, that guy was his father-in-law, and in most circles, decking your father-in-law was considered bad form. But, damn, he wanted to. He'd also wanted to shout that if in a year Chelsea wanted him to stick around, dammit, he was going to stick around, and there was *no* amount of money in all the world that would convince him to do otherwise.

He grabbed a glass of champagne off a tray as a server went past, then turned to look for Chelsea.

He found her almost instantly. She was standing out on the sundeck, leaning against the railing, sipping a sparkling water and talking to Benton Scott.

"They look good together, don't they?"

Johnny glanced up to see Chelsea's brother Troy standing next to him, watching his friend and his sister through the glass in the French doors. They did look good together—both slim and blond and elegant.

"Bent told me just yesterday that he and Nicole have finally called it quits. He filed the divorce papers last week." Troy looked questioningly at Johnny. "I'm sorry—what was your name again?"

"It's Johnny," he answered flatly, then added, "Does everyone know?"

"That you're not Emilio? Pretty much. It's hard to keep a secret in this family, especially one of that magnitude." Troy laughed. "It was funny how it slipped out, actually. The real groom—I mean, the *former* groom—had a mutual friend who knew my brother Michael, and that friend kind of let slip the news that Emilio was getting married next month to a girl from Greece, and Michael thought, gee, that's odd, this is the same guy who just married my little sister. Not long after that the cat was totally out of the bag." He paused for breath. "So I hear Grandpa went overboard with the amount he left for Chelsea. What's your share?"

"That's not your business," Johnny said evenly.

"I'll find out sooner or later, but suit yourself." Troy turned to look at Chelsea and Bent. "I think those two are going to end up together—you know, after she divorces you."

Johnny tried to stay cool despite the fact that with every beat of his heart, rage-heated blood was surging through his veins. Somehow, again, he managed to stay silent, and after a moment Troy faded away.

As Johnny watched, Chelsea gave Bent a smile and walked toward the house. The man's eyes followed the soft sway of her hips, and Johnny knew that if it were up to Benton Scott, he'd steal Chelsea back in a heartbeat. He swore silently. Could this situation possibly get any worse? Chelsea's family obviously thought Johnny was beneath her, her father had tried to buy him off, and now the man whom she confessed had at one time been the love of her life was clearly interested in rekindling their romance.

He had a sick feeling that when he got home and finally went through yesterday's mail, he was going to find a notice of an impending IRS tax audit. The day was going *that* well.

But then Chelsea spotted him, her eyes warm with pleasure. She hadn't looked at Benton Scott that way, had she?

But instead of coming over to him, she took a left turn as she approached, veering away from him and toward the front hallway. She glanced back over her shoulder, gesturing slightly with her head for him to follow her.

Johnny set his glass down on a passing server's tray and trailed slightly behind her. In the entryway, she went quickly up a flight of thickly carpeted stairs, glancing back again to see if he was following.

"What's up here?" he asked, taking the stairs two at a time to catch up with her at the top landing.

She put her finger on her lips in a gesture of silence and looked carefully down the hallway in either direction. She glanced back down the stairs, then she stepped into a dark doorway, pulling him with her and shutting the door behind him.

Johnny laughed as she locked the door, and just like that, his unpleasant conversations with Chelsea's father and brother were instantly worth it. Johnny literally had to hold his tongue between his teeth to keep from telling her, right then and there, how deeply he loved her.

Because they were in the bathroom. Out of all the places they could have gone to talk privately, Chelsea had chosen this one because she knew it would make him laugh—and make him wonder if she was bold enough actually to make love to him with the party going on downstairs. He was wondering. Boy, was he wondering. He pulled her into his arms and kissed her, but she pulled away.

"My sister told me everyone knows you're not Emilio," she told him, "but my father hasn't said anything to me yet."

"He said something to me," Johnny told her.

Chelsea winced, her blue eyes filled with worry. "I'm so sorry. Was it awful?"

"It was...educational," he said diplomatically, deciding not to tell her about her father's offer of money. He didn't want to talk about what was going to happen when this year was over. He didn't want Chelsea even thinking about it until she had a real chance to see that being married to him wasn't a threat to her independence. He didn't want to talk about it until she'd gotten used to him being around, and maybe—please, God—even loved him a little. "But I survived intact."

Chelsea ran her hands up his chest and down his shoulders. "Maybe I should check, just to make sure."

Her touch had the power to make him crazy, so he pulled away slightly, needing to look into her eyes as he asked a question he knew he shouldn't ask. "I saw you talking to Benton Scott. Did he tell you he's getting divorced?"

She gazed back at him. "He did. Apparently it's been rather nasty. He wanted to have lunch sometime this week to talk about it."

Johnny felt his insides twist. He kept his face and his voice carefully neutral. "Oh?"

"What do you think?" she asked. "Should I go?"

Both her voice and the pure wideness of her eyes were far too innocent, and Johnny realized she had worked very hard to hide the smile that now slipped out.

"Only if you want me to kill him," he told her.

Her smile turned into a laugh of disbelief. "Oh, my God, you *are* jealous!"

"I can't help it," he admitted. "I know your history with this guy and..." He caught her beautiful face between his hands and looked searchingly into her laughing blue eyes. "I need to hear you tell me you don't want him anymore."

"I don't want him anymore," Chelsea said. "I stopped wanting him the first time you kissed me." She smiled at him, bewitchingly. "I think you know what I do want, though. It has something to do with you and me and the guest bathroom during one of my parents' parties..." Her smile turned to a grin, heat and devilment sparkling in her eyes. "I believe the expression is: Put up or shut up."

Pulling her into his arms, giddy with relief and desire, Johnny did both.


"He was really jealous of Bent. That's a good sign, isn't it?"

Moira looked at Chelsea in obvious exasperation as she poured the grounds for their morning pot of coffee into the filter. "Have you asked him how he feels? When grown-ups want to know how other grown-ups feel, they usually *ask*."

"I *know* how he feels. He likes me. He *really* likes the physical side of our relationship. But the biggest attraction for him is the money he's going to get when the year is over." Chelsea closed her eyes. "Sierra called to tell me that Daddy offered Johnny a huge amount of money—provided that at the end of the year he really does divorce me and disappear."

"And Johnny didn't mention that to you?" Moira added water and clicked the coffeemaker on.

"Nope."

"Ouch."

"Yeah."

"In that case, okay, I can understand why you might not want to take the risk of telling him that you love him."

Chelsea sighed, gazing out her window at the early-morning sunshine already warming the city street. "I have a year to figure out how to make him fall in love with me."

"A lot can happen in a year," Moira said reassuringly.

"Maybe if I offer him even *more* money, he'll stay," Chelsea said morosely. "God, I can't believe I just said that."

In the outer office, the bell tinkled. Someone had come in.

"Hey, how'd they get in without buzzing?" Moira asked, frowning. The building had an outer door that locked. People coming into the offices had to be screened through an intercom before they were buzzed in.

"The lock's not working again," Chelsea said. "At least it wasn't when I came in. I already called the landlord."

"Are you expecting a client?" Moira asked.

Chelsea shook her head. "No." Her heart leaped. Maybe it was Johnny, stopping in after his Meals on Wheels rounds. It was still a little early, but maybe ... Eagerly, she pushed herself out of her chair and followed Moira into the outer office.

"Hey!" she heard Moira say in outrage. "What do you think you're doing?"

The man rifling through the drawers of Moira's desk definitely wasn't Johnny.

He was ragged and dirty, his short hair matted against his head, his face streaked with grime as if he'd slept, facedown, in the back alley. His hands were shaking and his eyes were red and tearing. He looked up, teeth bared in a growl of anger and frustration that made him seem more animal than human, an enormous handgun tightly clenched in one trembling hand. "Where the *hell* is your cash register?"

Chelsea's heart was pounding, but she spoke calmly as she gently took hold of the waistband of Moira's pants and slowly, an inch at a time, began backing them both away from that deadly looking gun. "We don't keep any money here. This is an *office*, not a retail store. We don't have a cash register."

"You're lying," he bit out. He needed both hands to hold the gun steady, he was shaking so badly. He turned suddenly, and fired three fast, deafening shots that shattered the front window. Chelsea couldn't hold back a scream as Moira crumpled in a dead faint.

"Show me where the freakin' cash register is, or I'm going to freakin' *kill* you!" the man shouted.

---

Finding a big enough parking spot around the corner from Chelsea's office, Johnny pulled the Meals on Wheels truck into it, feeling particularly triumphant. His luck had been right on all day. Even Mr. Gruber had seemed much better, upbeat and cheerful for all of Johnny's visit.

And now he was going to drop in on his wife, see if he couldn't talk her into going home with him for an early lunch. Lunch, and maybe a little nonfood refreshment...

He rounded the corner, a definite jaunt in his step, but then stopped short.

There were three police cars and an ambulance haphazardly parked in the middle of the street, as if they'd arrived in a big hurry and skidded to a stop. Uniformed officers were crawling all over the place, going in and out of the building.

A crowd had gathered, and someone had put out yellow crime-scene tape, keeping them back—away from the main door to the building Chelsea's office was in.

It was the yellow tape that did it, the yellow tape that sent Johnny's heart into his throat and twisted his insides into a knot. He'd grown up in a part of town where he'd seen that yellow tape too often, and nine times out of ten, when that yellow tape appeared, there was a dead body or two to go with it.

Johnny broke into a run, and as he got closer the fear that was gripping his chest tightened its grasp as he saw the entire front window of Chelsea's outer office had been broken from the inside out. Jagged shards of glass littered the sidewalk.

He pushed through the crowd and slipped under the yellow tape, only to come face-to-face with a cop the size of a professional wrestler. "Where do you think you're going, pal?" the man demanded roughly.

"My wife works in there." Johnny pointed to the office beyond the broken window. He could barely get the words out, his throat felt so tight. "What happened? Was anyone hurt?"

"I don't know yet," the cop told him, sympathy in his eyes, moving aside to let him pass. "I'm just working crowd control. All I know is gunshots were fired and someone called the ambulance."

Gunshots fired. Ambulance.

Johnny took the stairs up to the door three at a

time, bracing himself for the worst, preparing for the scenario that he dreaded finding—the woman he loved, her life snuffed out, lying in a pool of blood.

For the first time since his mother had died, Johnny found himself praying.

Several plainclothes detectives were standing and talking with several uniformed officers. But there was no sign of Chelsea—dead or alive.

"I'm Chelsea Spencer's husband," he nearly shouted at one of the police officers. "Where is she? Is she all right?"

"She's one of the women who worked here?" the policeman asked.

"Yes."

"Then she's with the paramedics," the policeman told him, "in the back office. Someone was hurt, but I don't know who. Junkie came in, needing a fix, went ballistic with a gun."

"Oh, my God." The door to Chelsea's office was closed, but Johnny went toward it anyway, intending to knock it down if he had to, imagining Chelsea lying there, in her office, bleeding to death while the paramedics stood nearby, unable to save her.

But he didn't have to knock the door down, because before he got there, it swung open.

And Chelsea was standing there. "Johnny? I thought I heard your voice."

She was alive. She was whole. Unbloodied. Unhurt.

Johnny reached for her, holding her tightly, unable to breathe, unable to hear from the rushing of the blood in his head, unable to see from the blur of tears that filled his eyes, unable to say anything but her name.

She held him just as tightly as he lifted his head and kissed her.

It wasn't a kiss of desire, although there was always a spark of passion each time their lips met. It was more a kiss of affirmation, a kiss of possession, a kiss of gratitude. It was a kiss that drove home to Johnny all that he would have lost had Chelsea been killed today, and it pushed him beyond his limit.

Holding tight to Chelsea, Johnny wept.

"Johnny, my God..." He could hear the surprise in her voice.

"I'm sorry," he said, laughing at himself, but unable to stop the flow of tears. "God, when I saw that yellow tape, I thought..." His laughter became a sob and he kissed her again, harder this time, molding her body against his own, uncaring of who saw them kissing, and who saw him crying.

He let her pull him into her office. Moira was there, lying on the sofa, an ice pack on her head and a paramedic sitting at her side, taking her blood pressure and pulse.

Chelsea pushed him down into the chair behind her desk and then sat on his lap.

Johnny took a deep breath, closing his eyes and letting his head rest against the softness of her breasts. He felt her hands in his hair, her fingers soothing. God, talk about losing it.

When he finally opened his eyes, she was looking down at him, her expression so sweet, her eyes so tender. Yeah, he'd lost it, but she didn't seem to mind.

He wiped his face with his hands, took a deep breath, forced a smile and tried to joke. "Let me get this straight. *You're* the one who was face-to-face with a strung-out gunman, but *I'm* the one who's being comforted. What's wrong with this picture?"

"Excuse me, Ms. Spencer." One of the plainclothes cops was standing in the door and Johnny and Chelsea both looked up. "If it's possible, we'd like to ask you some questions now."

"I have a few questions of my own." Chelsea slid off Johnny's lap. "I thought I overheard someone say you caught the man with the gun—is that true?"

"Yes, ma'am. A suspect similar to the one you described to the 911 operator was apprehended carrying a firearm." The police detective stepped into the room. He was an older man, slightly overweight, with thinning hair combed futilely over a bald spot. But his eyes were sharp as he gazed at them and around the room, seeming to miss no detail. "What we'd like is to get your statement, and then take you down to the station, to ID the suspect in a lineup."

"Will that take long?" Johnny asked.

The detective focused a pair of cool gray eyes on Johnny. "Are you the husband?"

Johnny stood up, holding out his hand. "Yeah. Giovanni Anziano."

The detective clasped his hand. "Detective Paul White. It shouldn't take more than fifteen minutes, tops."

But Chelsea was shaking her head. "I can't just

leave Moira here. And what about the broken window? Anyone could just walk right in and take our computers."

Moira's voice drifted thinly from the couch. "My brother's on his way over. He's going to drive me home. I could ask him to come back and make sure the window gets boarded up."

"I can take care of that," Johnny volunteered. "No problem. But before you go anywhere, I want to know what the hell happened."

"The lock on the outer door was jammed again," Moira told him, "and this guy just walked right in. We heard the bell when the door opened, and when we came out into the outer office, he was searching through my desk, looking for money."

Chelsea spoke up. "He had one of those giant Dirty Harry guns."

"The perp we picked up was carrying a .44 Magnum," Detective White murmured.

"He kept asking where we kept the cash register," Moira said. "And when we told him we weren't a retail store, that we didn't have a cash register, he freaked, and fired at the windows, and started really screaming at us. That's when I did my Perils of Pauline routine and fainted. But

Dudley Do-Right wasn't around to catch me, so I hit my head on the way down."

"I'm sorry I didn't catch you," Chelsea told her friend.

"You were a little busy trying to figure out how to keep the wacko from slaughtering us," Moira said dryly. "Personally, I think you made the right choice by ignoring me."

Johnny gazed at Chelsea, unable to keep from picturing her standing there, all alone, one-on-one with a man who probably wouldn't have hesitated to kill to get the money to buy him the drugs he needed.

"I was standing there, looking down the barrel of that enormous gun," Chelsea said, her voice very soft, "knowing that this guy was going to kill me because we didn't have a cash register that he could rob. And then I remembered—the petty-cash drawer. I keep a purse in the bottom drawer of my desk with about two hundred dollars in cash for emergencies or COD deliveries or whatever. I told him the money was in the other office, and that there was also a back door he could use to get out of the building."

Chelsea took a deep breath. "I knew there was a

good chance he was going to get all paranoid about being caught, and that he would shoot me even if I gave him the money, but I was hoping that if I closed the door as we went into the back office, he would forget about Moira. So I gave him the money, and then I pretended to faint—I guess I figured maybe if I was lying on the floor, he might forget that he hadn't already shot me. I don't know, it just seemed like the right thing to do at the time, and when I opened my eyes again he was gone. That's when I called 911."

The police detective was taking notes on a small pocket pad. He looked up. "You were smart," he said. "And you were extremely lucky. This man's MO is almost identical to a robbery homicide that took place in Dorchester a week ago. Front window of the store shot out... Of course, three people were killed that time. Still, my money's on him being the same guy. We have prints from Dorchester—with any luck they'll match."

Johnny reached for Chelsea, pulling her into his arms. "God," he murmured. "My God."

Chelsea's voice shook. "May we go to the station now? I want to do this quickly so I can come back here and have my husband take me home."

Johnny didn't want to let go of her. "Sure you don't want me to come with you?"

She shook her head. "I need you to stay and take care of that broken window. I should probably call the landlord and—"

"Don't worry," he told her. "I'll take care of it. I'll take care of everything."

# FOURTEEN

CHELSEA COULDN'T BELIEVE her eyes.

Two workmen were on the sidewalk and two were inside the office, carefully lining up a pane of glass to replace the broken window.

She glanced at her watch as she got out of the police car that had driven her back. True, she'd been gone longer than she'd hoped, but it really hadn't been much more than an hour since she'd left Johnny to deal with the mess in the office.

Identifying the man who'd robbed her hadn't taken long. She'd picked him out of the lineup

without hesitating. It had been the paperwork afterward that had taken forever.

The lock *still* wasn't working on the outer door
as she went into the office. Johnny was on the
phone, sitting behind her desk, and he quickly rang
off when he saw her.

Chelsea pointed out toward the outer office and
the window. "How on earth...?"

Johnny smiled at her. "Rudy—you know, my
boss at Lumière's—his brother-in-law is best
friends with a guy whose son owns a glass-
replacement company. We got lucky, both that
they had a truck in the neighborhood, and that this
is a pretty standard-sized window." He stood up.
"Let me see how long these guys think they're
going to be. If they're going to be here for a while,
I'll take you home and then come back."

Chelsea followed him out into the outer office.
There were two police detectives dusting Moira's
desk for fingerprints, and a uniformed cop standing nearby, chatting with them. This office had
never been so busy. "Don't you have to be at the
restaurant pretty soon?"

Johnny shook his head. "I told Rudy I wouldn't
be able to get in until five at the earliest. I'll call in

later and tell the guys what to start chopping for the evening's special."

Chelsea looked at the window and the men working. "They're going to be done in just a few minutes. Why don't we just wait, that way you won't have to come back?"

"I'm going to have to come back anyway," Johnny told her, putting an arm around her shoulder and giving her a hug. "Someone needs to be here when the truck arrives."

"Truck?"

"Yeah. I arranged for a moving company to come out and pick up your computers and all the stuff in your desks and on your shelves," Johnny told her.

"What?" Chelsea was shocked. "And move them where?"

"To my condo. I figured we can bring the dining-room table into one of the spare bedrooms and set up a temporary office there and—"

"No way." Chelsea pushed away from him. "Absolutely not. That's *crazy*—"

"It would only be temporary," he said. "Until you found office space in a better part of town."

Her voice rose. "Johnny...God! We can't afford to be in a better part of town."

"You can't afford *not* to be."

"I can't believe you would just go and call movers without even asking me."

His voice rose too. "I can't believe you're even *thinking* about staying here after what happened!"

"Well, I *am* thinking about it. And the more I think, the more I'm convinced that we have to stay. We have a lease. If we leave we'll be breaking the lease, and we'll not only have to pay a higher rent, but we'll be slammed with a lawsuit and forced to pay the rent on this place too. Not to mention all the time we'll waste searching for some mythical office that's both safe *and* affordable."

Johnny's eyes were bright with anger. "Money," he said. "That's what it always comes down to for you, Chelsea, doesn't it? What's it going to cost you? Well, let me tell you something, babe. There's no dollar amount in the world that's worth you risking your life for. If you get sued by this scumbag landlord, *I'll* pay. And *I'll* pay the difference between what you're paying now and the higher rent on a place with a doorman and real locks on the door. Jesus, in a year we're both going to have more money than we could spend in a lifetime! As far as I'm concerned, whether or not you should move your office was not a question that required any asking. You're outta here, as of today. I don't give a damn what your landlord says, or even what *you* say, for that matter."

Chelsea couldn't believe what she was hearing. "I'm not going anywhere, so you can just call those movers back." She looked around, suddenly aware of the police officers and the window repair crew who were listening with unabashed curiosity. "This is obviously not the time to discuss this," she said icily.

Johnny was furious, and the sudden appearance of the Ice Princess didn't help calm him any. "When will it be time to discuss it?" he asked. "After the next guy with a gun breaks in and this time blows a hole in your head?"

"I will not talk about this now." She stalked haughtily back toward her office, and he caught up with her, pushing open her office door and holding it for her.

"You want privacy? Fine. Let's go in here, close the door, and talk about how much of your precious money you plan to spend on security to make this place safe enough." Johnny closed the door behind her, watching as she stiffly moved to stand with her arms folded across her chest, staring out the window. "Let's talk about the fact that this guy didn't stumble in here in the middle of the night. Let's talk about the fact that it was ten o'clock in the morning when he held that gun in your face."

She turned to face him and her eyes were cold, her expression carefully distanced. "I'm sorry, this decision is not yours to make," she said icily. "It's my decision, and I'm not going anywhere."

Johnny wanted to scream. Didn't she know that just the thought of her coming back here to work tomorrow made him sick to his stomach? Didn't she know that the fear he'd felt when he'd first seen that yellow tape was not something he could just forget overnight? Didn't she know that he loved her more than any dollar amount, more than his own life? "Wanna make a bet? I already made the decision—the movers are on their way."

Two bright spots of pink appeared on Chelsea's cheeks, but she covered her anger with a thick layer of frost and spoke more softly rather than shouting. "Your name's not on this lease along with mine—"

"No, but my name's on a marriage license along with yours." It was the wrong thing to say. Johnny knew that it was the wrong thing to say, but once he started he couldn't seem to stop. "You're my wife, and I *will not* allow you to come here anymore. Why am I even bothering to talk to you about this? This is *not* a topic that is open for discussion."

The Ice Princess facade wavered, then crumbled as Chelsea's anger became too strong to hide. "You won't *allow* me to stay?"

"Damn straight."

"Just because you think you're my husband, you're ordering me to just pack up and run away—"

"I don't just *think* I'm your husband. I *am* your husband."

"Like hell you are." She was shaking, she was so mad. "Get out."

"I'm not going anywhere. I'm waiting for the truck, remember?"

Her movements jerky, Chelsea gathered up her purse and jacket, her laptop and her briefcase and started for the door. "Fine. Then I'll get out. You'll hear from my lawyer. This stupid game has gone far enough."

"Oh, so now it's a stupid game?"

She turned to glance at him over her shoulder as he followed her quickly down the hall, out of the office, and onto the sidewalk. "Marriage has always been a stupid game. And I was a fool to think you'd play by smarter rules."

"Smarter rules. *Your* rules, you mean. What about *my* rules? What about what *I* need?"

There were tears in her eyes as she lifted her hand to hail a cab. "You need my money. And my father's money. Don't look so surprised. Did you really think I didn't know he'd sweetened our deal? Between the two of us, you'll have enough for your restaurant. That's all you really want, anyway."

And just like that Johnny's anger was deflated. "Is that really what you think?"

A taxi pulled to a stop in front of her.

"I can't talk to you right now," Chelsea said with a sob, opening the cab door. "I have to go home."

"Let me drive you."

"No." She closed the door.

He leaned in the window. "Chelsea, we need to talk more. If you think all I need is that money, then we have to—"

"Go," Chelsea told the driver.

The taxi pulled away, taking with it Johnny's heart.

His condo was as silent as a tomb. Johnny knew before he even shut the door behind him that Chelsea wasn't there.

She'd gone home. To *her* place. *Her* home.

Dammit, he'd handled that all wrong.

After Chelsea had left he'd called and canceled the movers. He wanted her to move, but now that his anger had faded, he knew that making demands and doing it against her will was not the way to go. She had to make the decision to move on her own, not have it forced down her throat.

Johnny picked up the phone and dialed her number in Brookline. No answer. He was about to leave a message on her machine when he heard the sound of a key in the lock.

As he hung up the phone the front door opened, and Chelsea came in. She was dressed in jeans and a T-shirt, her hair back in a ponytail. She looked like a teenager, sweet and impossibly young. She stopped short at the sight of him, glancing quickly at her watch.

"No," he said. "You're right. It's after five. I'm supposed to be at work."

She was clearly ill at ease. "I just, um..." She moistened her lips. "I wanted to get my stuff."

Johnny felt his heart break. "That's it? You're just gonna pack up your things and leave?"

"This whole thing was such a big mistake, and—" She turned back to the door. "I don't want to talk, John. Not now. You're already late for work—"

"I went in earlier," he told her quietly. "I got everything set up and ready to go. I told Rudy I needed the night off—to try to save my marriage."

She looked up at him at that, her eyes bruised looking in the paleness of her face. "Johnny—"

"I know. You don't want to talk. You don't have to talk—you just have to listen, okay?"

"I heard more than enough this morning," she said softly.

"No, you didn't. You heard too much and too little, all at the same time. Chelsea, look, I know I was wrong to make the demands I did." He held her gaze steadily, praying that she would believe him. "I said some things I shouldn't have, I went a little crazy on you, and I'm sorry about that. But I need you to give me a chance to explain why finding office space in a safer part of town is so important to me."

Johnny took a deep breath. So far, so good. So far she was listening, and that's all that he could ask. He glanced at Chelsea's watch, reading the time upside down and backward. It was five-fifteen. The timing was perfect. He couldn't have planned this better if he'd tried. "I'd like to show you something," he continued. "Will you go for a ride with me?"

But Chelsea was shaking her head no, opening the door, about to walk out of his life, maybe forever. "I can't."

"Please," he said. "Chelsea, I heard you out. That day you asked me to marry you? I could've walked away from you, but I didn't. I listened to what you had to say. All I'm asking is for you to give me the same chance."

She closed her eyes in defeat. "Oh, God." She took a deep breath and looked up at him. "I'll give you fifteen minutes."

Johnny nodded. "That's all I need."

Chelsea sat in the front seat of Johnny's VW Bug. "Where are we?"

"We're in a part of Boston you've probably never been to before," he told her with a wry smile. "We're a few blocks away from the Projects. This is where I grew up."

Chelsea gazed out the window. The dreaded Projects. Funny, she'd always imagined a bombed-out, burned-down landscape with deserted buildings and trash in the streets. But this neighborhood was nice. There were flowers growing in window boxes, the sidewalks were swept, and a carefully tended playground where children played and laughed was nestled between two apartment buildings.

Johnny pulled over to the side of the road, squeezing the little car into a tiny parking spot. "I can't come down here without thinking about my mother," he continued. He got out of the car and came around to open Chelsea's door. "She was an advocate against urban violence. She was one of the leading forces in the community pride program too."

He led her down the sidewalk, toward the corner, where they stood, waiting for the light to change. "She started all kinds of neighborhood watch programs, and cleanup programs, and afterschool programs. She helped clean out the basement of her health clinic and turn it into a rec center for teenagers. I spent a lot of time there myself."

The traffic slowed before the walk light came on, and Johnny stepped out into the street. Chelsea hurried across after him, wondering if her nervousness at being in this part of the city showed. Didn't drive-by shootings happen down here regularly?

But Johnny didn't seem to notice her nervousness. He was still talking about his mother. "But there was one program she started that she wished to God she hadn't had to set up. They had their first meeting more than fifteen years ago, and they're still meeting once every two weeks, here at the church."

Chelsea looked up and realized she was climbing the steps that led up to the front doors of a stately looking brick church.

Johnny fell silent as he opened the door for her

and they went inside. She followed him down a flight of stairs to the cool mustiness of a church basement. He led her down a long, dimly lit hallway, where there were a number of little darkened Sunday-school rooms off to either side. She could hear voices coming from a room way down at the end, but that room, too, seemed dark.

As they approached the double doors she saw that the room was quite large. The overhead lights had been turned on only for the far side of the room, creating an area of light bordered by the late-afternoon dimness.

A group of about thirty people sat in a circle illuminated by that light. One of them was speaking as the others listened. The mood was solemn and the tone of the voice speaking was sad.

Chelsea stood next to Johnny, in the shadows. "What is this?" she whispered.

"It's a support group for people who've lost a child or a parent or a spouse to urban violence," he whispered. "Listen, okay?"

"I should have been home," a woman was saying, her voice tearful. "Or I should have somehow taught her not to open the door for anyone. Not for *anyone*. I should have spent more time with her, teaching her things like that. And I keep thinking about all those times I was too tired or too busy or too wrapped up in figuring out how to pay the bills to play with her. I keep thinking about all those times that I didn't take the time to give her a hug and tell her how much I loved her...."

"I think that's something we all feel," another woman said, her voice stronger, clearer than the first. "This sense of wasted opportunity, this sense of wishing we'd been a little more aware of how precious life is, and how quickly it can be taken from us. I think we all wish we had one more chance to tell our loved ones that they were, indeed, loved."

A man spoke up. "My wife was killed four years ago by a car being chased by the cops. As I was watching her casket being placed into the ground, I couldn't remember the last time I told her that I loved her. I tried, but I just couldn't remember. It may well have been years. And I remember thinking, sweet Jesus, I'll never have another chance. So now I tell our daughter and son how very much I love them every single day. And I like to believe that somewhere up in heaven, LaRae can hear me." He laughed, but it was laughter filled with sorrow. "She always did have good ears, that woman. I like to believe she knows I'm talking to her too."

"I love you, Chelsea," Johnny whispered.

Startled, she turned to look at him. Despite the shadows, she could see the shine of tears in his eyes.

He tried to smile. "That's why I want you to move your office out of that part of town," he told her softly. "That's why it's so important to me that you're safe. I know damn well that you could've died today, and then I would've spent the rest of my life sitting in a group like this one, filled with regret that I never told you that I love you."

He loved her. Johnny Anziano *loved* her.

"Oh, my God," she said, forgetting to be quiet, and across the room, a number of heads turned toward them.

"May I help you?" one of the women called out.

"No," Johnny said. "No, thank you. I'm sorry we disturbed you."

"Johnny Anziano, is that you?" another woman asked.

"Yeah," he said. "How are you, Mrs. Samuels?"

"It's Dr. Anziano's boy," Mrs. Samuels told the others. "Who's that with you, Johnny?"

"This is my wife. Her name is Chelsea," Johnny told them.

"Your *wife*!" a man called out. "Congratulations, young man!"

"Thanks, Mr. Hart."

"What are you doing out this way?"

Johnny hesitated. "I wanted to . . . show Chelsea the church."

"The sanctuary's open, sweetie," Mrs. Samuels said. "Just go on up."

"Thanks, Mrs. S. Sorry to interrupt your meeting."

Chelsea let Johnny lead her out of the room and up a flight of stairs. He loved her. He *loved* her. "Everybody knew you." Somehow her voice sounded normal when she spoke. How had she managed to do that?

"About ten years ago I was tapped to join a gang," Johnny told her, "and when my mother found out, she made me sit in on these meetings. Needless to say, it was an eye-opener."

Johnny opened a set of doors and they stepped into the church.

The late-afternoon sun was shining through the stained-glass windows, giving the sanctuary an otherworldly, shimmering glow.

She followed him down the aisle and up toward the altar.

"I always thought if I ever got married, I'd be married here, in this church," Johnny said. Even though he spoke softly, his voice seemed to echo in the stillness.

He turned to look at her then. The ghostly light cast shadows, but even they couldn't disguise his face—a face she'd come to know so very well over the past few short weeks. His eyes were lazily hooded, as ever, and, as ever, they seemed to gleam with an intensity that was far from lazy.

"I don't want to join one of those support groups, Chelsea," he told her. "I don't want to sit in that circle and cry while I talk about losing my wife. I know I said some things to you this afternoon that I shouldn't have. You're right. Even though you're my wife, even though we're married, I don't have the right to tell you what you can or can't do. But I do have the right to ask. So I'm asking. Please, *please* move your office to a better part of town. I'll beg, if you want. I'll crawl if that'll make you understand how important this is to me. I need to know you're as safe as you can possibly be."

Chelsea couldn't speak. Her heart was in her throat.

"I know you were surprised when I told you that I love you." He cleared his throat. "And I don't have a clue what you're thinking, but don't freak out, because I know that falling in love wasn't part of our deal, and I know that you're in this marriage thing for only a year, and I swear, I'd never hold you to anything more, and even if you don't want to stay with me, I'm not going to take that money from your father and... Okay, now I'm babbling." He took a deep breath. "At least tell me you forgive me."

"I forgive you," she whispered. "Promise you'll try not to do it again?"

He nodded, tears again gleaming in his eyes. "Please," he said again. "Let me help you move your office somewhere safer. Please, Chels. If you care for me even just a little bit..."

"I do," she said. "I will. Move the office. But I *will* need your help—"

He stepped toward her. "You know you've got it. I promise."

"What I really want you to promise me..." Chelsea had to stop and blink back her own tears. "Promise me you'll love me forever."

She saw disbelief flash in Johnny's eyes. "Do you want me to?"

"Yes," she whispered. "More than anything."

The disbelief turned to sheer joy. He laughed aloud, then raised his voice so his words rang out in the church. "Then, yes, I promise."

"For richer or poorer?"

Johnny held out his hand to her, again letting his words echo. "I do promise."

"For better or for worse?" She slipped her hand into his, and it felt like coming home.

The look in his eyes was one she'd seen there before. When she'd woken up in the middle of the night and found him gazing down at her, when he thought she didn't see him watching her from across the room—that was love she'd seen in his eyes. He truly loved her.

"I do," he told her.

"In sickness and in health?"

"Yes. For as long as we both shall live," he said.

"I love you, Johnny," Chelsea said. She smiled at him through her tears. "I think you better kiss the bride."

Johnny was nervous. He knew he shouldn't be. He knew he held the upper hand, along with the element of surprise.

He stood up as Howard Spencer came briskly out into the waiting area.

"Why don't you come on back into my office," the older man said, leading the way to a huge corner office with a gorgeous view of downtown Boston that was almost as good as the view from Johnny's condo. "I have the contracts all drawn up for you to sign."

Johnny waited until Mr. Spencer had closed the door behind him. "Actually, Mr. Spencer, I have no intention of signing your contracts, because I have no intention of taking your bribe. As a matter of fact, I came here today to tell you that your daughter and I have come to a new agreement. We've removed the end date from our relationship and hope to have as long and as happy a marriage as you and Julia have had."

Howard Spencer was not the kind of man who sputtered, but he was as close to sputtering now as he ever had been.

"Also—for your information—I've made Chelsea sign an addendum to our prenupt, saying the financial deal's off. I made her sign an agreement saying that her money is her money, and my money is *our* money." Johnny smiled. "I know, I know, you're thinking, if she ever leaves me, I'm going to get royally screwed, but you know what, Mr. S.?"

Howard Spencer seemed unable to respond.

"She's never going to leave me. I'm going to do my damnedest to see that Chelsea stays madly in love with me for the rest of our lives. Because I love her that much. Look at me and read my lips, Mr. S. I love your daughter. There's no amount of money in the world that would make me walk away from her. I'm going to make her happy—and that's what you want for her, right? For her to be happy? Nod your head. Yes."

Howard Spencer managed to nod his head. Yes.

Johnny smiled again. "Then I'm your man. We're on the same team now, Howie."

He turned to leave, but then turned back. "Oh,

I almost forgot." He lowered his voice conspiratorially. "This conversation? And the one we had previously? They never happened."

Johnny walked out of the office, but then stuck his head back in the door. "One more thing. Chelsea and I would love for you and Julia to join us for dinner Friday night—in Lumière's private dining room. Chelsea tells me you haven't had any luck getting a reservation for the private room—I don't know why. But from now on, when you call, tell 'em you're Johnny Anziano's father-in-law." He winked. "*That'll* get you in."

# EPILOGUE

CHELSEA COULDN'T BELIEVE what she'd found.

She'd been looking for a spare book of stamps in Johnny's desk, thinking if she found one, she wouldn't have to pull on her boots and trudge out into the snow, shovel out her car, and drive through the slushy streets to the post office vending machines.

She hadn't meant to pry. But the envelope was right there, top slit open, sitting next to the computer. The return address said it was from the International Culinary Institute in Paris.

Johnny had told her he'd get a response to his

application for the Paris study program by December. And it was definitely December.

Chelsea picked up the envelope and held it up to the light, which of course revealed nothing. She put the envelope down and picked up the phone, pressing the speed dial for Lumière's.

Johnny answered on the fifth ring. "Anziano."

"Hi," Chelsea said. She held the envelope up to her nose and smelled it. It smelled like paper. "Are you busy?"

"For you? Never. Well, almost never. What's up?"

"That's what I was going to ask you," Chelsea said, tapping the envelope on the edge of his desk. "What's up?"

Johnny laughed. "Didn't *you* call *me*?"

"Yes, but, I was just..." Chelsea sighed. "We've both been so busy lately, we haven't had as much time to talk, and..."

"Well, let's see. Jean-Paul's wife is pregnant again—have I told you that?"

"Yes," Chelsea said. "Yes, I think you mentioned that last week." She tapped the envelope on her teeth.

"Your father called me again—he wants to back me in whatever kind of restaurant I want to open."

"Don't even *think* about—"

"I made polite, vague noises. Don't worry about that. Let's see.... You knew that my latest tofu recipe was getting a huge write-up in *Vegetarian Times*. I saw the article today—it's *great*. I'll bring it home for you. They're calling me the 'Tofu Gourmet.' There's been a huge demand for the dish here at the restaurant—I just wish tofu weren't so damn *ugly*. But that's all I can think of. Nothing else is new. Hang on a sec." There was a pause, and Chelsea heard muffled voices, as if Johnny had put his hand over the mouthpiece of the phone. "I'm sorry, Chelsea, I gotta go. I'll try to get home early tonight, okay?"

"Johnny—"

"I love you, Chels."

"Wait!"

But he'd already hung up.

Chelsea slowly put the handset back in the cradle of the telephone and looked at the envelope she was still holding. Nothing else was new?

She couldn't help herself. She pulled the letter out and opened it and...

Dear God, he'd been accepted.

She skimmed the page, then went back and read the next-to-last paragraph. Dear God, he'd not only been accepted, but he'd been asked to *give* a seminar on his new specialty—gourmet cooking with tofu. It was an honor beyond compare.

The letter was dated October 25. Even if it had been sent via surface mail, Johnny must have gotten it weeks ago. Longer.

Yet he'd said nothing about it to her.

Feeling a total sneak, Chelsea turned on Johnny's computer and accessed his word-processing program. It didn't take her long to skim his list of files and find one labeled Paris.ICI. She clicked on the job and, saying a silent pray asking forgiveness from the God of Nosiness, opened it.

*Dear Admissions Committee,*

 *It was with great pride that I received your letter requesting my presence as part of your Paris study program this May. And it is with great regret that I inform you that I am unable to attend for the full three months. I understand that—*

Chelsea clicked out of the job. She'd seen enough.

Unable to attend. Regret.

Oh, God, Johnny was turning down the chance of a lifetime—because of her.

Oh, God, this was her worst nightmare come true. There was no way she could leave Spencer/O'Brien Software in May for three months.

But it didn't matter anymore. He'd turned the opportunity down. Without even *talking* to her.

Chelsea turned off Johnny's computer and went to pull on her snow boots.

Johnny was preparing the fourteenth order that afternoon for his tofu dish when Chelsea burst into the kitchen.

"I need to talk to you. Now." She then added the word they'd promised each other they'd always use, even when they were upset. "Please."

Johnny nodded to Philippe, who took over his pan of sautéing vegetables. "Let's go into my office," he said, but she was already heading there. What had he done? He couldn't think of a single thing. Maybe it had something to do with that weird phone call she'd made just a little while ago. He closed the door behind him. "Are you mad at me?"

"Yes, I'm mad. And I'm hurt, and upset, and disappointed and sad and—"

"What? Why? Chelsea, wait a sec, I'm clueless here. What's this about?"

She smacked him in the chest with an envelope. Johnny fumbled, but caught it before it hit the ground. He recognized it immediately.

"How could you not talk to me about this?" Chelsea looked ready to cry. "How could you just turn down their offer without even telling me?"

"How do you know I turned down their offer?"

"I searched for your return letter on your computer." She was too upset to be embarrassed.

Johnny had to laugh. "But you didn't read the whole thing, did you?"

"I read all that I needed to."

Johnny pulled her into his arms. "Chels, if you're going to be nosy, don't be nosy halfway—or you'll get only half the story. The letter I faxed them said that *at this time* I couldn't stay the full three months, but I proposed that I attend for a few weeks to give the seminar they requested. I asked if I could postpone taking part in the full three-month program until next year. I'm waiting for their response."

She looked sheepishly up at him. "I didn't read that far."

He kissed her. "No kidding."

"Johnny, why didn't you tell me about any of this?"

"I was waiting to hear back from ICI before I told you. It seems like a good compromise, don't you think?"

"What if ICI says it's now or never?"

Johnny shrugged. "By May, you'll have the money from your trust. You can fly me home for weekends—I don't know. We'll figure something out."

"We can compromise," Chelsea said. "You can fly home for some weekends, I can fly to Paris for others. We can definitely make this work."

As Johnny gazed into Chelsea's ocean-blue eyes he knew she was right. Together, with compromise, they were unstoppable.

Johnny smiled, and then kissed his wife.

# about the author

Since her explosion onto the publishing scene more than ten years ago, SUZANNE BROCKMANN has written over forty books, and is now widely recognized as one of the leading voices in romantic suspense. Her work has earned her repeated appearances on the *USA Today* and *New York Times* bestseller lists, as well as numerous awards, including Romance Writers of America's #1 Favorite Book of the Year—three years running, in 2000, 2001, and 2002—two RITA awards, and many *Romantic Times* Reviewer's Choice Awards. Suzanne lives west of Boston with her husband, Dell author Ed Gaffney. Visit her website at www.SuzanneBrockmann.com.